Echoes of the Forgotten

Once Upon Historians series, Volume 2

Danika Prasad

Published by Danika Prasad, 2024.

This is a work of fiction. Similarities to real people, places, or events are entirely coincidental.

ECHOES OF THE FORGOTTEN

First edition. December 1, 2024.

Copyright © 2024 Danika Prasad.

ISBN: 979-8230126072

Written by Danika Prasad.

Also by Danika Prasad

Once Upon Historians series
Echoes of the Forgotten

Standalone
Meanwhile, Elsewhere
Invitation to Paris
Once Upon Historians
Meanwhile, Elsewhere

Table of Contents

Prologue...1
Chapter 1: Shadows at the Funeral..4
Chapter 2: Something Was Off...13
Chapter 3: The Unthinkable...24
Chapter 4: Echoes of Deception...34
Chapter 5: Bound to Delhi..42
Chapter 6: Into the Unknown..49
Chapter 7: Family Ties..55
Chapter 8: Unbroken Bonds...64
Chapter 9: A Walk with Nana..73
Chapter 10 – Journey to Agra..79
Chapter 11: Wisdom in Old Friendships....................................86
Chapter 12: The Last Day...93
Chapter 13: The First Flight Back... 100
Chapter 14: The Next Flight.. 107
Chapter 15: The Rest of the Flight.. 115
Chapter 16: The Meeting... 120
Chapter 17: The Examinations.. 127
Chapter 18: On Duty.. 135
Chapter 19: The Unexpected Knock on the Door.................. 142
Chapter 20: The Gathering.. 148
Chapter 21: Investigation.. 155
Chapter 22: The Turnaround.. 161
Chapter 23: The Results... 166
Chapter 24: The Revival.. 171
Chapter 25: The Reunion.. 176
Chapter 26: Legal Action Against the Wongs........................ 181
Chapter 27: Peace at last.. 187

Prologue

In the quiet aftermath of tragedy, life gathered into the solemn embrace of the chapel. The morning sun broke through the grey, casting sharp light across rows of black-clad figures. Today, they came together to bid farewell to a man who had shaped their lives in ways both grand and subtle—Dr Zayd Hasan. He had been more than just a renowned academic; he had been a mentor, a friend, and for many, a symbol of the pursuit of truth.

The day of his funeral marked a turning point. For those gathered, it was a moment heavy with grief but also tangled in the memories of his final years. Zayd had fought a battle with cancer, a slow erosion of his once robust intellect and spirit. His death was not sudden, but the finality of it weighed heavily on each heart present.

Samira, his eldest daughter, stood quietly at the front. Her face was a mask of composure, the same look she had worn through the long months of her father's illness. Beside her, Sara shifted her weight, biting her lip, as if trying to find the right way to grieve. Their mother, Evelyn, sat between them, a widow lost in thought, eyes fixed on the polished casket as though searching for the right moment to speak, to mourn, or to collapse under the weight of her loss.

Nearby, Mrs Laila Khalil—Dr Hasan's elder sister—sat in silence, her husband Laila close by, a pillar of strength. Their sons, Omar and Rami, had flown in for the occasion. Omar, the meteorologist, glanced at the sky as though reading the weather for the funeral, while Rami, the doctor, stood stiff and professional, not as a nephew, but as a physician who had seen death too many times before.

But their grief, deeply personal as it was, did not stand alone. As the small church began to fill, familiar faces gathered to mourn and remember. Elodie Laurent, Naureen Mehra, and Kanchana Desai—the trio of historians whose lives Zayd had touched so deeply—slipped quietly into their seats. The years had changed them, but their bond remained strong, forged through shared study, endless debates, and the kind of adventure only history could provide. They had become like a second family to Zayd, and he to them.

Elodie's eyes darted around the room, taking in the details of the sombre scene. Kanchana sat beside her, quiet for once, hands folded in her lap, while Naureen leaned forward, elbows on his knees, as if searching for some sign or understanding in the slow-moving proceedings. In their minds, Zayd was still the brilliant teacher who had opened doors to mysteries long forgotten. His death left a hollow space, a silence where once there had been endless conversation.

And then there were the three newcomers. Unfamiliar faces in a sea of memories. Danya Agarwal, Mia Armstrong, and Mira Quaid arrived quietly, yet with purpose. They weren't strangers, not entirely. Their presence had been anticipated, though it remained unspoken. The message Kanchana had left for them after hearing of Zayd's death brought them here, drawn to the past they shared. Each was an ENT surgeon, yet beyond their profession, they shared something deeper with the historians—memories of their younger days, moments when their paths had crossed with Zayd's and Laila's family in unexpected ways.

Danya, Mia, and Mira walked down the narrow aisle of the church, eyes scanning the faces of the mourners. They were greeted with nods from the historians, recognition from the Khalils, but otherwise remained unnoticed by many. Their connection was not to the immediate family, but to a time long ago, a time when they, like Elodie, Naureen, and Kanchana, had been drawn to the Hasan family by a shared passion for discovery.

In those earlier years, they had all been close, bound together by their professions and by their shared love of history and medicine. Danya, always the cautious one, had taken the lead in reconnecting after Kanchana's message. She had known that Zayd's death would draw them together again, just as it had years ago when they were younger, and their careers had only begun to intertwine. Back then, their reunions had been more frequent, sparked by chance encounters, research symposiums, or simply the magnetic pull of shared interests.

Mia, the boldest of the group, had needed no convincing. Her admiration for Zayd and Laila had only grown with the years, and despite the distance between them all, she felt a deep sense of obligation to be present for his final farewell. Mira, perhaps the quietest, followed them without question, knowing that her place was among these faces, some familiar, some from her past.

The trio's arrival marked a quiet yet significant moment in the service. They took their seats at the back, out of sight, but not out of mind. Their connection to the past was just as real, just as deep, though many in the room might not remember it. As the priest began to speak, reciting the traditional words of comfort, the minds of those gathered drifted through the past, each recalling different versions of the same man, different moments, different truths about who he had been.

The truth—the real truth, as it would come to be known—was buried deeper than even Zayd's most well-guarded secrets. And though today was about closure, about saying goodbye, it was also the beginning of something else. As the service moved forward, unnoticed threads of the past began to weave together, unseen yet undeniable.

Zayd's death was not the end of his story. There were still mysteries to uncover, questions to ask, and truths to reveal. And for those who had gathered, whether family, historian, or friend, the Journey was far from over.

In the silence of the church, as the final prayers were offered, there was a sense of calm. But for those who truly knew Zayd Hasan, there was something else Beneath it all—a quiet anticipation, a recognition that though his body would rest, the truth was still out there, waiting to be uncovered.

And so it begins again.

Chapter 1: Shadows at the Funeral

The chapel remained heavy with silence after the closing prayer. Zayd Hasan's coffin sat at the front, a quiet reminder that the man who had shaped so many lives was now gone. The mourners lingered, hesitant to leave, each locked in their private thoughts. Conversations in hushed tones drifted through the aisles, while others remained still, absorbing the weight of the moment.

At the back, unnoticed by most, the historians—Elodie, Naureen, and Kanchana—sat together, eyes scanning the room. They had come to pay their respects, but there was an unease in the air, something they couldn't quite place. Beside them, Danya, Mia, and Mira—the ENT trio—shifted in their seats, exchanging uneasy glances. The sense of loss bound them all, but there was a tension simmering just Beneath the surface.

The doors of the chapel creaked open, breaking the stillness. A pair entered, their footsteps echoing loudly against the floor, drawing the attention of everyone inside. Alex and Anya Wong—a brother and sister so sharp in their movements they cut through the atmosphere like a knife. The air in the room shifted immediately.

Alex, broad-shouldered and impeccably dressed, led the way with Anya by his side. Her thin lips curled into what could only be described as a smirk, her eyes narrowing as she surveyed the room, clearly unimpressed by the sombre faces around her. They strode confidently, unapologetically, down the aisle as though they owned the place. Eyes turned toward them, recognizing the interruption, but nobody moved. The tension rose instantly, a ripple of unease spreading through the mourners.

The Wong siblings were notorious—especially to those who had gathered for Dr Hasan's funeral. They had a history here, a bitter one. The tension between the Wongs and the rest of the group, especially the historians and the ENT trio, ran deep. During their school years,

Alex and Anya had been more than just a thorn in the side of Zayd's students and colleagues—they had been bullies. Ruthless, relentless, and proud of it.

Elodie stiffened as they approached, her eyes locking on the siblings. Naureen clenched his jaw, his gaze lowering to the floor, trying to keep his composure. Kanchana, usually the first to crack a Lake in tense situations, remained silent, her hands gripping her lap tightly. Across the aisle, Danya, Mia, and Mira glanced at each other, their faces hardening with recognition. They, too, had felt the sting of the Wongs' cruelty.

"Look who decided to show up," Alex said, his voice sharp and mocking, cutting through the quiet like broken glass. "The good doctor's funeral. How... touching."

Anya followed her brother's lead, her eyes scanning the rows of mourners with disdain. "Honestly, I'm surprised any of you bothered to show up. A man like him? Finally dead. You should be celebrating."

The gasp from the crowd was audible. Faces turned, shock and confusion mixing in the air. Evelyn Hasan, Zayd's widow, turned sharply in her seat, her face pale, unable to process the words that had just pierced the solemnity of the service. Her daughters, Samira and Sara, exchanged tense glances, caught between grief and outrage.

The Wongs moved closer to the front, ignoring the murmurs and the icy stares that followed them. Their presence seemed to drain the warmth from the room, replacing it with something far colder.

"You've got some nerve," Naureen muttered under his breath, his hands tightening into fists, knuckles white. His voice was low, but Elodie and Kanchana heard it clearly, the anger bubbling just Beneath the surface.

Danya leaned toward Mia and Mira, her voice barely a whisper. "What are they even doing here? They hated Zayd."

"They hated all of us," Mia added, her eyes never leaving the pair as they made their way to the front. "Remember what they did to Kanchana?"

Kanchana bit her lip but said nothing. The memories were too close, too sharp. Years of taunts, of cruel pranks, of Alex and Anya turning every day into a game of survival for anyone who crossed their path.

Alex reached the front of the room and turned to face the mourners, his smirk widening. "I'm just glad the old man's finally gone. Dr Zayd Hasan—what a Joke. Acting like he was some big deal, like he knew better than everyone else. He was nothing. And now? Now he's where he belongs."

The words cut deep, and the room seemed to freeze in response. The mourners, shocked into silence, didn't know how to react. Zayd had been respected, loved even, by those who knew him, but Alex's venomous words hung in the air, challenging anyone to speak up against him.

Anya stepped forward, her voice dripping with contempt. "You all sat here, listening to those stupid prayers, pretending like he was some kind of saint. Well, he wasn't. He was a pretentious old man, and he's better off dead. Just like his precious little students." Her eyes flicked to the historians and then to the ENT trio, her expression twisting into something darker.

"You really think we've forgotten?" Anya continued, her voice rising. "The way you all acted? So self-righteous, thinking you were special because Hasan and his family liked you. Teachers' pets, every single one of you. Pathetic."

Danya stood up, her voice firm and clear. "What the hell are you doing here, Alex? Anya? This is a funeral."

Alex turned to her, his smirk unfazed. "We're paying our respects, Danya. Isn't that what this is? A celebration of Hasan's life?" His eyes narrowed, and he stepped closer, his voice lowering but still loud enough for everyone to hear. "Besides, we wouldn't miss this for the world. Seeing you all here... grieving for a man who was just as pathetic as the rest of you... it's priceless."

The silence that followed was thick, the tension nearly unbearable. The entire room seemed to be holding its breath, waiting for someone to react, for someone to break the uncomfortable stillness. But nobody moved.

Anya's eyes flicked to Samira and Sara, her smile thin and cold. "I guess you two are next, right? After all, it's only a Matter of time before the Hasan legacy fades away completely."

Samira's face remained impassive, but her hands clenched at her sides. Sara, unable to contain herself, stood up sharply, her voice shaking with fury. "Get out. Both of you."

Alex laughed, a short, cruel sound. "Or what? Are you going to cry, Sara? Run to Daddy? Oh wait—you can't. He's dead."

Before anyone could react, Kanchana stood up. "Leave," she said, her voice stronger than anyone had expected. "This is a funeral. You don't belong here."

Alex's smile faltered for the briefest moment, but he quickly regained his composure. "Fine," he said, turning to leave. "But don't think for a second that we're done."

Anya followed him out, her parting words floating back into the chapel. "Good riddance to Hasan. The world's better off without him."

As the doors slammed shut behind them, the tension in the room remained. Silence hung thick in the air, but it was a different kind of silence now—a silence filled with anger, with grief, and with the undeniable presence of the shadows the Wongs had cast over them all.

And Beneath it all, a darker truth began to surface. A truth that Alex and Anya might have been right about one thing: Zayd was gone, but his story was far from over.

Danya's Diary

Today's funeral should have been a quiet farewell. It should have been a moment of reflection, of honouring a man who meant so much to me, to all of us. But it was anything but that.

I can't stop thinking about how everything unfolded. I suppose I knew, deep down, that funerals are rarely simple or peaceful. Grief, when it gathers so many people together, becomes unpredictable. People bring their baggage—emotional, historical, personal—and it all spills out in unexpected ways. But today, something else entirely overshadowed our grief for Zayd.

The Wongs.

Even as I sit here writing this, my hand still shakes from the fury they stirred up inside me. Alex and Anya Wong. I haven't thought of them in years. I had hoped I'd never have to think of them again. But there they were, walking into the church, like some twisted spectres from our past. They never belonged, not here, not with us, and yet they arrived as if their presence was a cruel Joke we were all supposed to understand.

From the moment they stepped through the doors, you could feel the tension. The weight of their disdain hung in the air, and everything that had been quiet and respectful turned sour. I still remember the way Alex smirked as he strode down the aisle, as though he was walking into a party, not a funeral. And Anya, with her cold, piercing eyes, scanning the room as if she was assessing how much damage she could do in the shortest amount of time.

Why were they there? They hated Zayd. They hated everyone who had ever been close to him (which were the 6 of us). The answer is obvious: they wanted to remind us of that hatred, to rub it in our faces on the day we were vulnerable. And it worked. Oh, how it worked.

The look on Samira's face when Alex spoke—I'll never forget it. She didn't say a word, but her expression... it was as if every bitter memory she had of those two came rushing back, all at once. I saw her knuckles turn white as she clenched her hands, holding on, barely. She stayed composed, but I could tell how much it cost her. I wish I could've said something, done something, before it all went to hell. But I was frozen, just like everyone else. The poison they spat at us, at Zayd—it was paralyzing.

"We should be celebrating," Alex said. Celebrating. Celebrating Zayd's death. How could someone be so cruel? How could someone stand in the place where we were supposed to mourn and turn it into... whatever that was?

It wasn't just about Zayd, though. Alex and Anya made sure to remind us all of what we had gone through with them. Their hatred wasn't just directed at Zayd—it was aimed at every one of us who had ever been close to him. Every time they turned their gaze on me, or Mia, or Mira... every time they sneered at Elodie, Naureen, or Kanchana... it was a reminder. A reminder of how they used to torment us, humiliate us, make our lives hell all those years ago.

God, the memories. They came flooding back in ways I wasn't prepared for.

Back then, it felt like we couldn't escape them. Alex and Anya seemed to thrive on making everyone else miserable. In school, they targeted the weakest among us—or at least those they thought were weak. And since we were the ones who had a good relationship with Zayd and Mrs Khalil—because we cared about history, about learning—we became their favourite targets. The "favourites," they called us, like we were the teachers' pets. I hated that term. I hated the way it made us feel like we were somehow different from everyone else, when all we were trying to do was survive in a system that felt like it was built to tear us apart.

But it wasn't just petty name-calling. Alex and Anya were far more calculated than that. They knew exactly how to find your weaknesses, how to dig under your skin and get to the parts of you that you didn't even know could hurt. I remember how they would taunt us, calling her out in front of everyone, making fun of her enthusiasm for history. They even called her "Little Miss Perfect" and "Hasan's Pet," always with that edge of cruelty that made it seem like an insult when it was nothing more than a reflection of her passion. Kanchana would brush it off with a Joke most of the time, but I could see it hurt her.

What about Mira and Naureen—they took a particular pleasure in getting under their skin. He was always so analytical, so thoughtful, but that made him an easy target. They'd mock his insights, twist his words around to make him seem arrogant. "Too smart for your own good," Alex would say, and the way he said it—like their intelligence was something shameful—was so infuriating. It broke all of us down over time, and I could see how it made Naureen question himself, question everything he said, even around us.

Elodie... oh, Elodie. She put up the strongest front, but Alex and Anya had a way of getting to her too. I remember the day they spread rumours about her, lies that were so vicious they almost tore her friendships apart.

And Mia! WOW! She stood strong through it all, but I knew it affected her. She never let them see how much it hurt, but I saw the cracks.

As for me, I thought I'd grown past it. Even I had to deal with the "Little Miss Perfect" and "Hasan's Pet". I thought I had left all that anger and frustration behind. But seeing them today, hearing them speak about Zayd like that—about us—it brought it all rushing back. Back then, they didn't just bully us. They made us feel like we didn't belong. Like everything we cared about—history, learning, being part of something bigger than ourselves—was ridiculous. They wanted to crush us, and sometimes, they succeeded.

I remember how it felt to be in the middle of their attention. I was always the quiet one, the one who tried to stay out of trouble. But that only made me a more appealing target. They saw my silence as weakness, and they exploited it every chance they got. The snide comments about my background, the whispers about how I didn't belong—those were the easy parts to deal with. It was the psychological games that wore me down. The constant questioning of my worth, the doubts they planted about whether I was smart enough, strong enough, good enough.

And today, when Alex looked at me with that same smug expression, it was like I was back there again, shrinking under their scrutiny, trying to make myself small so they wouldn't notice me. But they did. They always did.

Anya's voice today was just as sharp, just as cutting. She didn't even need to raise her voice to make her words hurt. I think that's what made it worse. The way she casually dismissed Zayd's life, and by extension, all of us who had been a part of it. "Good riddance," she said. Good riddance. Like he was nothing, like his life meant nothing. And not just his, but ours too.

I could feel Mia tensing beside me when Anya spoke. She's always been more outwardly bold than I am, but I could tell she was holding back. The same with Mira. It's funny—we've all gone on to do such important work in our fields, to help people, to make a difference, and yet, for that brief moment, it was like we were back in school, reduced to our teenage selves, powerless against their venom.

Kanchana was the one who stood up first. She had every right to, after all they'd done to her, but I was surprised by how strong her voice was. I shouldn't have been, though. Kanchana's always had a kind of quiet strength about her, one that most people don't notice until it's too late. She told them to leave, and for a moment, I thought they might. But Alex just laughed, that cruel, dismissive laugh that haunted me for years.

I couldn't stay silent anymore. I had to say something. It was Zayd's funeral, for God's sake. I couldn't let them ruin this too. I told Alex and Anya to leave, that they didn't belong here. It felt good to finally speak out, to say the things I never could back then. But even as I said it, I knew it wouldn't be the end of it. Alex's parting words, that smug promise that they weren't done with us—it was a reminder that this was far from over.

What struck me most, though, was how everyone reacted once they were gone. The room didn't breathe a collective sigh of relief. Instead, there was this lingering tension, this sense that their presence had stirred something up that wasn't going to go away just because they left. It was like they had planted a seed of doubt, of anger, and it was growing inside each of us. I could see it in the way Samira and Sara stood beside their mother, rigid and unyielding, refusing to break in front of the people who had hurt their father's memory. I saw it in Naureen's clenched fists, in Elodie's set jaw, in Kanchana's tight smile that barely hid her rage.

And in me? I felt it too. As soon as I got home, I wanted to scream and cry all my feeling. I still feel it now, sitting here, hours later, writing this down as if I can somehow exorcise the anger and frustration by putting it into words. But the truth is, I'm still furious. Not just at Alex and Anya, though that's part of it. I'm angry at the fact that after all these years, after everything we've accomplished, they can still make us feel like that.

Chapter 2: Something Was Off

The funeral had ended, but the weight of the day still pressed down on everyone. The sun had dipped lower in the sky, casting long shadows across the churchyard as people began to file out, quiet murmurs replacing the earlier atmosphere of grief. Zayd Hasan's death had hit hard, but what had happened during the service—the intrusion of Alex and Anya Wong—had left an even darker shadow hanging over those who remained.

Danya, along with Mia and Mira, stood off to the side of the church, just beyond the heavy stone steps. They had been part of the last to leave, their conversation carried on in low voices, punctuated by heavy silences. None of them could quite shake the feeling that something had shifted after the Wongs' abrupt exit. Something deeper, more unsettling, lingered.

"I still can't believe they came," Mia muttered, running her hand through her hair as she stared out at the grey horizon. "Of all people, why them? Why today?"

"Because they wanted to hurt us," Danya replied. "That's what they've always done. They came to take away whatever peace we had left."

Mira was silent, her gaze distant. She hadn't said much since they'd walked out of the church, but Danya knew her well enough to sense the tension building behind her calm exterior. Mira had never been the type to speak before thinking, but when she did speak, it was usually because she had something important to say.

"It feels like they came for more than just that," Mira finally murmured, her voice barely above a whisper.

Danya looked over at her, raising an eyebrow. "What do you mean?"

Mira hesitated, biting her lip. "I don't know. It's just a feeling. Something about the way they acted. They didn't just come to mock us or to spit on Zayd's memory. It felt... planned. Like they were waiting for this moment."

The words sent a chill through Danya. She hadn't thought of it like that, but now that Mira said it, she couldn't shake the feeling either. The Wongs had always been bullies, yes, but something about today had felt different. Calculated. Cold.

"Let's not give them that much credit," Mia said, though her tone lacked conviction. "They're just sadistic. Always have been."

Mira didn't respond, and the silence between the three of them grew heavy again. They had all endured the Wongs' cruelty in the past, each in their own way. It wasn't a time any of them liked to remember, but those memories had been dredged up by today's events, and now they felt fresh again—too fresh.

Danya was about to suggest they leave when she noticed something out of the corner of her eye. It was subtle, barely noticeable at first. A slight rustle of movement among the trees that bordered the churchyard. She turned her head, squinting into the gathering dusk, but saw nothing.

"What is it?" Mia asked, following Danya's gaze.

"I thought I saw something," Danya replied, her voice dropping a notch. "Over there."

Mia peered into the shadows of the altar, but she didn't seem convinced. "Probably just a bird or something. This place gives me the creeps, especially after today."

Mira said nothing, but she too was staring into the same direction, her posture tense.

The rustle came again, louder this time, a shuffling sound like something—or someone—moving through the brush. It was faint, but in the stillness of the evening, it stood out.

"There," Danya whispered, pointing. She wasn't imagining it. Someone—or something—was definitely there.

They all stood frozen for a moment, eyes locked on the grove of trees, waiting for whatever—or whoever—was hidden there to reveal itself. Danya's heart raced, her pulse quickening as the feeling of unease that had settled over her earlier deepened. The Wongs had already shaken her nerves, but now this? The timing was too strange.

"Maybe it's just the trees outside," Mia offered, though even she didn't sound convinced anymore.

"Or maybe it's not," Danya replied softly.

Before they could speculate further, the rustling stopped. The stillness that followed was even more unsettling than the sound itself. Whoever had been moving through the trees was now perfectly silent.

Danya exchanged a look with Mira, whose face had grown pale, her eyes wide with a tension that mirrored Danya's own. There was something deeply off about this. It wasn't just their imaginations. Someone was watching them.

Suddenly, Kanchana appeared from around the side of the church, her hands buried in her coat pockets as she approached. Her eyes darted between the three of them, immediately sensing the tension.

"What's going on?" she asked, her voice low.

"There's someone—or something—in the church," Danya said, her eyes never leaving the spot where the rustling had come from. "We heard it."

Kanchana glanced at the trees, her brow furrowing. "Are you sure?"

"We're sure," Mira said quietly, her voice carrying a weight that made Kanchana pause.

The four of them stood there, silent, waiting for any sign of movement. The wind had picked up, rustling the leaves now, but that earlier sound—deliberate, almost calculated—was gone. Whoever had been there was either hiding or gone entirely.

"Should we check it out?" Mia asked, but there was hesitation in her voice. They weren't exactly a group used to investigating strange sounds in the dark.

Before anyone could answer, there was another rustle, this time from the opposite direction, near the churchyard gate. It was softer, more distant, but enough to put them all on edge again.

"Okay, this is getting weird," Kanchana muttered, taking a step back from the trees. "What is going on here?"

Danya's mind raced. Could this be some twisted prank from the Wongs? It wasn't like them to use subtlety—they were more of the in-your-face type of antagonists. But that didn't mean they wouldn't be capable of something more elaborate, especially after the way they had stormed into the funeral earlier.

"I don't like this," Mira said, her voice tight. "Something feels wrong."

Danya agreed, but before she could say anything, Naureen and Elodie appeared, walking towards them from where they'd been speaking with Samira and Sara. They, too, seemed on edge.

"We heard you guys talking," Naureen said, his eyes narrowing as he joined them. "What's going on?"

"Something's out there," Danya said, gesturing to the trees. "We heard movement, twice now."

Naureen and Elodie exchanged a glance, their faces darkening.

"Do you think it's... them?" Elodie asked, her voice barely above a whisper.

"Alex and Anya?" Kanchana shook her head. "They're bold, but this feels... different."

"I don't know if it's them," Danya said slowly. "But whoever it is, they're not making themselves known, and that's what worries me."

For a few moments, they all stood in tense silence, eyes scanning the shadows, ears straining for any hint of movement. The churchyard, once peaceful, now felt like a trap, the stillness around them pregnant with something they couldn't name.

"Maybe we should go," Naureen suggested. "There's nothing here but bad memories tonight. And everyone is scared, especially Danya and Mira".

But just as he said it, there was another sound—a louder rustle, more deliberate this time, followed by a faint, unmistakable snap of a branch. It came from the thickest part of the tree line, just out of sight.

"That's it," Mia said, backing away quickly. "I'm not sticking around to find out what that was."

Mira, already pale, took a step back as well. "We need to leave."

They started to move toward the gate, but Danya lingered a moment longer, her eyes fixed on the spot where the sound had come from. She could feel her heart pounding, every instinct in her telling her to follow the others, to leave this place behind. But something held her back. Curiosity, maybe. Or fear. Or the nagging feeling that there was more to this than they understood.

And then she saw it—a flash of movement. Just for a second. A figure, barely discernible in the deepening shadows, slipped further into the trees. Whoever it was, they were deliberately staying out of sight. But they were there. Watching.

Danya's mind started spiralling out of control.

"Danya, come on," Mira called, her voice tense. "We need to go. You heard what Naureen said!"

Danya turned, finally tearing her gaze away from the trees. She nodded and quickly followed the others through the gate. Her mind was racing, her body still tingling with adrenaline. As they made their way toward the car park, the feeling of being watched didn't leave her.

None of them spoke as they reached their cars, the quiet between them thick with unspoken tension. The Wongs had already made the day unbearable, but now this? It was too much.

As they started to say their goodbyes, a sense of dread settled over Danya. This wasn't over. Whatever—or whoever—had been in the trees, it wasn't random. It wasn't just some animal or a trick of the wind.

Someone had been watching them, and she had the sinking feeling it wasn't the last time they'd encounter this kind of unease.

Later that night, as Danya sat in her quiet house, her husband and 2 children asleep, the day's events kept replaying in her mind. She was afraid of how she was going to tell her husband and children about the situation.

Danya's Diary

It's been hours since the funeral ended, but I can't stop thinking about it. My mind is racing, circling around everything that happened today—the words, the looks, the threats. But it's more than that. There's something deeper, something gnawing at the back of my mind.

Something's wrong. And I can't shake the feeling that it all leads back to Alex and Anya Wong.

Their appearance at Zayd's funeral was unsettling enough, but it's not just about what they said. It's the way they said it, the smugness, the certainty in their eyes. They wanted us to know they were still here, still looming over us, still capable of causing harm.

I keep replaying their words in my head, over and over again, especially what Anya said: "You two are next." Was that just a cruel taunt, or was there something more to it? The way she looked at Samira and Sara when she said it... it felt deliberate, like a threat wrapped up in mockery. As if Zayd's death wasn't the end of their twisted little vendetta. As if it were just the beginning.

And now, I can't help but wonder... were they involved?

It's ridiculous, right? People don't just go around causing cancer. But still, something feels off. Zayd had been battling laryngeal cancer for months, no wonder he was coughing and struggling too much! While I know how these things go, I also know enough about medicine to understand that strange coincidences often aren't coincidences at all. And there's something about the timing of all this—his sudden decline, the Wongs' reappearance at the funeral—that's making me question everything.

What if they didn't just come to gloat over his death? What if they were involved somehow, behind the scenes? I've heard of people doing terrible things to get revenge, to hurt those they hate. And Alex and Anya—they've always been cruel, but this feels like a different level of cruelty. A level that scares me.

I know I shouldn't jump to conclusions, but the thoughts won't leave me alone. Maybe it's paranoia. Maybe it's just grief clouding my judgment. But I can't shake the feeling that Zayd's death wasn't as simple as it seems.

I need to talk to someone about this. I can't keep these thoughts swirling in my head alone—it's driving me crazy. Mia and Mira would understand. They've known the Wongs as long as I have, and they were just as affected by today's events. They'd listen. Maybe they'd tell me I'm overthinking it, but I need to hear it from someone else.

What about Rami? He's a GP—he might have insight that I'm missing. Maybe he noticed something about Zayd's condition that didn't add up. Samira would be very significant. She was closer to Zayd than any of us, and as a paediatric consultant, she might see things differently. If there's even the slightest chance that something was off with Zayd's medical history, I need to know.

But how do I even mention this? How do I ask if they think Alex and Anya might have had something to do with Zayd's death without sounding insane?

Maybe it's not about asking outright. I could start by talking about Zayd's illness, how quickly it progressed, and see if anyone else noticed anything strange. If I frame it around the medical side of things, it won't seem so out of the blue.

Yes. That's what I'll do. I'll ask Mia, Mira, Rami, and Samira to meet up, maybe over dinner or something casual, and we can talk about it. I'll bring my laryngoscope and silicone mouthpiece to Naureen. From there, Mia can hand her biopsy kit to Kanchana and Elodie. It'll look like we're just going over medical stuff, nothing too serious. But once we start talking, I'll steer the conversation toward Zayd and his cancer. See what they think. Maybe they've had the same suspicions I have but didn't know how to voice them.

It sounds like a decent plan in my head. But I can already feel my nerves building up. What if they think I'm overreacting? Or worse, what if I'm right, and Zayd's death isn't as straightforward as we've all been led to believe?

I don't know which scares me more—the possibility that I'm wrong, or the possibility that I'm right.

But I have to find out. I owe it to Zayd, to myself, and to everyone who loved him. If there's even a chance that the Wongs were involved in some way, I can't just let it go. I need answers.

And then there's the other thing—what happened at the churchyard after the funeral. The rustling in the trees, the feeling of being watched. I know we all heard it. I know I wasn't imagining things. But who could it have been? Alex and Anya had left by then. Or had they?

The more I think about it, the more it feels like they could've been lurking, waiting, watching us. It's exactly the kind of thing they would do—something subtle, something to make us uneasy, to remind us that they're still out there, still capable of getting under our skin. And they succeeded. They've been in my head all day, and now I'm overthinking everything.

I wonder if Mira and Samira are thinking about it too. I should text them. Maybe they've had the same thoughts, the same feelings. I'm not the only one who felt that something was off today. There's no way.

I grab my phone and hover over Mira's name in my contacts. What do I even say? "Hey, I think the Wongs might have something to do with Zayd's death"? No. That sounds insane.

Maybe I should just start with the churchyard, mention how strange it felt, see if she picks up on it too. I type out a message:

"Hey Mira, I've been thinking about what happened at the churchyard today, with that noise in the trees. Did it seem off to you too? I can't shake the feeling that something wasn't right."

I hit send and immediately feel a knot tighten in my stomach. Now I wait. I type a similar message to Samira, careful to frame it around the churchyard and not dive into my deeper suspicions just yet.

"Samira, I wanted to check in with you. After your dad's funeral, did you feel like something was strange? When we heard that noise near the coffin... I don't know. It felt off. I'm probably overthinking it, but I wanted to ask."

I hit send again and lean back, staring at my phone. What am I even expecting them to say? That they agree with me? That they feel it too? Or that I'm just being paranoid and need to let it go?

The truth is, I don't know if I can let it go. There's this sinking feeling in my gut that's been growing since the moment Alex and Anya walked into the church. It's more than just grief. It's more than anger. It's like a knot of dread, something pulling at me, telling me that the Wongs are still involved in all of this, even now.

I think about everything they've done to us over the years, the way they used to manipulate and bully us. They always knew how to play the long game, how to get under your skin and make you doubt yourself. And that's exactly what they're doing now.

I catch myself spiralling, my thoughts spinning out of control. I take a deep breath, trying to calm the rising panic in my chest. I can't let them have that power over me again. I need to stay focused, to gather facts, not feelings.

That's why I need to meet with Mia, Mira, Rami, and Samira. If there's something medically off about Zayd's death, Rami will know. And if there's anything historically odd—patterns in the way laryngeal cancer develops, or something about the timing—Samira might be able to spot it. And I trust Naureen and Kanchana to look into whatever we find with fresh eyes, without letting emotions cloud their judgment.

I just need to stay rational. Logical.

But the Wongs... I can't stop thinking about them. The way they looked at us, like they still held all the cards. Like they knew something we didn't.

What if I'm not wrong? What if they *did* have something to do with Zayd's death? What if this is all part of their plan, and we're walking right into it without even knowing?

I'm not ready to confront that possibility, not yet. First, I need to talk to the others, to see if they've noticed anything I've missed. Then, maybe, we'll start to piece things together.

I just hope I'm wrong.

But I don't think I am.

Chapter 3: The Unthinkable

Danya sat at the head of the table, her fingers pressed against her temples as she stared down at the sheets of paper spread out before her. Notes, charts, medical diagrams—they were all there, meticulously arranged in front of her, but none of it eased the gnawing sense of dread that had taken root inside her since the funeral. The others were sitting in silence around her, their faces a mix of concern and curiosity, waiting for her to speak.

They had all gathered here, in this small, dimly lit room that Danya had chosen specifically for its privacy. After days of overthinking, sleepless nights, and constant anxiety, it had come to this moment—finally sharing her plan with the others. She knew it was a long shot. Hell, she knew it was insane. But she couldn't shake the feeling that they were missing something, something crucial about Zayd's death. She couldn't sit by and do nothing.

"So," Danya began, breaking the silence at last. "You're all probably wondering why I called you here."

Laila Khalil—Zayd's sister—sat at the far end of the table, her posture stiff but her expression neutral. She hadn't said much since the funeral, but Danya knew she was grieving in her own way. It was hard for everyone to process the loss of Zayd, but Laila had been a rock for so many people, even in her own pain.

Across from Laila, Naureen, Elodie, and Kanchana exchanged glances. Naureen leaned forward, elbows on the table, eyes fixed on Danya. Elodie sat back in her chair, arms crossed, as though bracing herself for whatever was about to come. Kanchana, ever calm in tense situations, gave Danya a small nod, as if silently urging her to continue.

To Danya's left, Mira, Mia, and Rami sat in quiet anticipation. Samira and Sara, Zayd's daughters, were on her right, both looking sombre, their faces betraying the exhaustion that came with both mourning their father and handling the sudden influx of unresolved questions about his death. Omar Khalil, Zayd's eldest nephew, was the only one who didn't seem tense, his arms folded as he leaned back against the wall behind the group, surveying the room.

"Since the funeral, I've been... thinking," Danya said carefully, choosing her words with precision. "Thinking about everything that's happened, everything we've seen. Zayd's death, it—it wasn't normal. I mean, of course, he had laryngeal cancer, but something about the way it all happened—it doesn't sit right with me."

Samira, ever composed, narrowed her eyes slightly. "What do you mean by 'not normal,' Danya?"

Danya took a deep breath, then continued, "I mean the progression of his illness. Laryngeal cancer is serious, yes, but even with the diagnosis and the advanced stage... there were some things that just didn't add up. The speed of the decline, for one. I've been going over everything in my mind, looking at the medical history, and something feels off. And then there's the Wongs."

She paused, letting the weight of that name settle over the room. Immediately, the tension grew thicker. Everyone knew the history, knew what Alex and Anya Wong had done to them all over the years. But now, bringing them into this conversation felt almost too far-fetched. Almost.

Laila's eyes flickered, her gaze hardening at the mention of the siblings. She had been around long enough to know the extent of the Wongs' cruelty, but even she seemed to question where Danya was headed with this.

"Are you suggesting that Alex and Anya... had something to do with Zayd's death?" Laila finally asked, her voice low and cautious.

"I don't know for sure," Danya admitted, her voice trembling slightly, "but I can't shake the feeling that they were involved somehow. I know it sounds crazy, but think about it—why did they show up at the funeral? Why did they go out of their way to mock us, to mock

Zayd's death? And the way Anya said, 'You two are next' to Samira and Sara... it felt like more than just a cruel taunt. It felt like a threat."

Sara shifted uncomfortably in her chair, but Samira's expression remained unreadable, her fingers interlacing as she rested her hands on the table.

"And that's why we're all here," Danya continued. "I've been thinking about this nonstop, and we need to investigate further. We need to look into Zayd's death, not just accept that it was the cancer. There could be more to this, and if the Wongs are involved, we have to find out."

Naureen let out a long breath, leaning back in his chair as he processed Danya's words. "So what exactly are you proposing?"

Danya hesitated, glancing at the equipment she had placed on the nearby table. This was the part that she had dreaded, the part where her plan went from theory to reality.

"I want to perform a post-mortem examination," she said bluntly.

The room fell into an immediate silence, everyone's eyes widening in shock. Danya could feel the weight of their reactions pressing down on her, but she pressed on.

"I know how this sounds, and I know it's not... typical. But we need answers. And I think the best way to get those answers is to examine Zayd's body. Look for any signs that something else may have caused or accelerated his death. Something that we missed before."

Elodie frowned, her arms still crossed tightly. "You want to do this in secret? Without the authorities?"

Danya nodded. "It's the only way. If we involve the authorities now, we won't have control over the process. And if the Wongs are involved, who knows what they could influence or cover up? We need to do this ourselves."

Laila was the first to speak again, her voice steady. "You're asking us to desecrate my brother's body."

"No," Danya said firmly. "I'm asking us to find the truth. Zayd would want us to know what really happened to him, Laila. He dedicated his life to uncovering the truth, and if there's even a chance that something more sinister was involved in his death, we owe it to him to uncover it."

Laila stared at her for a long moment before looking down at her hands, her expression unreadable. Danya wasn't sure if she was going to agree or walk out of the room. But after a tense silence, Laila finally nodded, a slow and deliberate motion.

"You're right," she said quietly. "Zayd would want the truth."

Danya felt a rush of relief wash over her, though she knew this was just the first step. There were still others who needed convincing.

Naureen and Elodie exchanged a glance, clearly conflicted. Kanchana, however, was already on board. Danya could see it in her eyes.

"I'm in," Kanchana said, breaking the silence. "If there's even a chance that we can find something, I want to help."

Naureen sighed, running a hand through his hair. "I don't like this. But I trust you, Danya. If you think this is the right thing to do, I'll support it."

Elodie didn't speak right away, but after a few moments of consideration, she gave a sharp nod. "Fine. But this has to be done carefully. We can't risk damaging anything that might be evidence."

Danya turned to Samira and Sara next. Of all the people in the room, they had the most at stake. If this went wrong, if they found nothing or if they found something they couldn't handle, it would only deepen the pain they were already feeling.

Samira spoke first. "I don't know if I believe in this theory, Danya. But if there's a possibility, however slim, that we missed something, then we have to do it. For Dad."

Sara nodded in agreement, though she seemed more hesitant. "I just don't want this to make things worse. If we do this and find nothing..."

"I understand," Danya said softly. "But if we find nothing, at least we'll know we did everything we could."

Finally, Danya turned to Mira, Mia, Omar, and Rami. Mira had always been the most cautious of the group, and Danya could tell this was weighing on her heavily. But Mira nodded, her voice calm but resolute.

"I'll help. We can't let fear stop us from finding out the truth."

Mia, ever the pragmatist, shrugged. "It's not exactly how I imagined spending my evening, but if this is what we need to do, I'm in."

Rami, the GP and the one who had perhaps the deepest understanding of Zayd's illness, was the last to speak. He looked down at the table, deep in thought, before finally lifting his gaze to meet Danya's.

"If this is what you need to do, I'll support it. But we have to be sure we know what we're looking for. If there's something off, we need to be precise. One wrong move could mean we lose any potential evidence."

Omar, Zayd's nephew, stood up and crossed his arms. "I'll help too. But I agree with Rami—if we're doing this, we need to be smart about it."

Danya took a deep breath and begun explaining the procedures.

Danya's Diary

I can't believe what we're about to do. Every part of me is screaming that this is wrong, but the stronger voice in my head—the one I can't ignore—keeps telling me that we have to do this. I can't shake this feeling, this overwhelming sense that we're missing something important about Zayd's death, and that the Wongs are involved. I know it sounds insane. I've spent every waking minute these past few days questioning myself, wondering if I'm overthinking everything, but I keep coming back to the same thought: something is off.

After the funeral, I couldn't stop thinking about that moment—when Alex and Anya walked into the church like they had every right to be there, like they owned the place. And then those words, the ones that keep looping in my head: "You two are next." It wasn't just a cruel taunt. I know it wasn't. There was something else behind those words—something dark, something calculated.

I've tried to push it aside, tried to tell myself that it's grief messing with my head, that I'm just looking for someone to blame. But this nagging feeling won't leave me alone. I can't get rid of it. I've replayed everything over and over in my head, trying to make sense of it. And that's when I came to the unthinkable conclusion: we need to investigate Zayd's death ourselves.

I know how this sounds. Hell, I know how it must have sounded to the others when I told them my plan today. Asking them to desecrate Zayd's body, to use medical equipment to examine him in secret—it's beyond insane. But what choice do we have? If we go to the authorities, they'll dismiss us. They'll call it a conspiracy theory. And the Wongs... they're too smart for that. If they're involved in this—and I really believe they are—they'll find a way to cover their tracks, to make us all look like we're losing our minds.

I've been thinking about Zayd's cancer, the way it progressed. I know enough about medicine to understand how aggressive laryngeal cancer can be, but there were signs that something wasn't right. The speed of his decline didn't match the typical progression of the disease. There were gaps in the timeline, unexplained symptoms. And now that I'm looking back on it, I'm wondering if we missed something—something crucial. I can't help but think that the Wongs had a hand in this. Maybe it's paranoia, but I can't let it go.

So, I decided. I called everyone together—Laila, Naureen, Elodie, Kanchana, Mira, Samira, Sara, Mia, Omar, Rami. We met in that small, dim room, away from any prying eyes. As I laid out the details of what I was proposing, I could feel their scepticism, their discomfort. I could see it in the way they glanced at each other, the way they avoided my eyes at first. But I pushed through, explaining why we needed to examine Zayd's body ourselves, why I thought we had missed something. I explained how I couldn't shake the feeling that the Wongs were involved. And then, slowly, one by one, they agreed to help.

Kanchana was the first to support me. She's always been the one who can see through the chaos, who can find the clarity in the midst of uncertainty. When she said she was in, it felt like a lifeline, like maybe I wasn't completely losing my mind. Naureen and Elodie followed soon after, though I could tell they were both hesitant. Naureen, especially, didn't like the idea of going behind the authorities' backs, but he trusts me. He knows that I wouldn't suggest something like this unless I truly believed it was necessary.

Samira and Sara... that was the hardest part. How could I ask them to go through this after everything they've already been through? How could I ask them to be a part of something so invasive, so painful? But Samira, ever pragmatic, agreed. She said she needed to know, that if there was even the slightest chance that we had missed something, she couldn't live with herself if we didn't investigate. Sara wasn't as sure, but she trusts her sister, and in the end, she agreed too.

Laila... well, Laila's face was unreadable the whole time I was talking. I couldn't tell what she was thinking, couldn't tell if she was angry or heartbroken or both. When she finally spoke, I wasn't sure what to expect, but she surprised me. She said Zayd would want us to find the truth, no Matter what it took. That was the moment I knew we had her blessing, and it felt like a weight had lifted off my shoulders.

Mira, Mia, Rami, and Omar all agreed in their own ways. Mira's always been cautious, but she understands the stakes here. Mia's always been more pragmatic, and Rami... well, Rami's a doctor. He understands better than anyone what we're up against medically. Omar, being Zayd's nephew, took a bit more convincing, but in the end, he agreed that we had to try.

Once they were all on board, we moved to the practical side of things. I had brought the equipment we'd need: Mira's otoscope and tongue depressors for Naureen, my own laryngoscope and silicone mouthpiece for Kanchana, and Mia's biopsy kit, which I handed to Elodie. It felt surreal, laying everything out like this, like we were preparing for some clandestine operation. And in a way, I suppose we are.

The plan is simple enough, in theory. We'll go to the funeral home after hours. I've arranged it so we'll have access to Zayd's body—thank God for old friends in the medical community who don't ask too many questions. Once we're there, we'll examine him as thoroughly as we can, looking for any signs that something unusual might have contributed to his death. If we find anything, we'll figure out our next steps. If we don't... well, at least we'll know we tried everything.

But I can't stop overthinking it all. What if we're wrong? What if there's nothing to find? What if this whole thing is just my grief twisting itself into paranoia? What if we desecrate Zayd's body for no reason at all? I don't think I could live with that. But what if we're right? What if the Wongs really did have something to do with this?

What if they're watching us right now, waiting for us to slip up, to make a mistake? What if they come after us next?

It's the thought that's been eating away at me since the funeral. The way Alex and Anya acted—it wasn't just about cruelty. It was about control. They've always thrived on making us feel powerless, and right now, I feel like we're playing right into their hands. Every time I close my eyes, I see their faces, hear their laughter. I can't help but wonder if they're enjoying this, knowing that we're unravelling, that we're starting to doubt everything we thought we knew.

I haven't stopped thinking about that night in the churchyard either, the rustling in the trees, the sense that we were being watched. At the time, I thought maybe it was just my imagination, but now... I don't know. It feels like something more. I've texted Mira and Samira about it, just to see if they've been feeling the same unease. Mira's always been more level-headed than I am—she'll tell me if I'm being paranoid. But even she seemed unsettled at the funeral. There's something about the timing of all this, the way the Wongs reappeared after being gone for so long, that makes me think this isn't over. Not by a long shot.

And then there's the equipment handover itself. It felt almost ceremonial, passing the tools we'll use to examine Zayd's body into the hands of people I've known and trusted for so long. Naureen took Mira's otoscope and tongue depressors without hesitation, though I could see the concern in his eyes. Kanchana accepted my laryngoscope and silicone mouthpiece, her face unreadable as she held the tools in her hands. And Elodie, with her usual calm confidence, took Mia's biopsy kit, nodding at me in silent understanding.

We're all in this together now, for better or worse. We've crossed a line, and there's no going back. I just hope we find something. I hope we're right. Because if we're wrong... I don't know how we'll live with ourselves.

I keep trying to picture what's going to happen when we finally do this—when we examine Zayd's body. I imagine us standing there in that sterile room, the lights too bright, the air too cold, and Zayd lying there, silent, as we search for answers he can no longer give. It feels wrong, in every way. And yet, it also feels like the only thing we can do.

I've been overthinking this whole situation, running every possible scenario through my mind. What if we find something that links back to the Wongs? What if we don't? What if, by some terrible twist of fate, we're putting ourselves in danger just by asking these questions? I feel like we're standing on the edge of a precipice, and one wrong move will send us all tumbling into a place we won't be able to climb out of.

I wish Zayd were here. He always knew how to make sense of things, how to find the truth in even the most complicated of situations. He would have known what to do. But he's not.

Chapter 4: Echoes of Deception

The air in the dimly lit room buzzed with tension as Danya surveyed her team. Shadows flickered across the walls, the overhead lights casting an ethereal glow on the medical equipment spread across the table. This wasn't just another meeting; it was a pivotal moment in their quest for truth. They were about to conduct an unauthorized examination of Zayd Hasan—an act that could change everything.

Danya cleared her throat, drawing everyone's attention. "Thank you all for being here. I know the stakes are high, but we can't allow Zayd's death to be treated as just another statistic." She felt the weight of their shared grief, but it was mingled with something else—an urgent need for answers.

Elodie shifted in her seat, her eyes flickering to the assorted tools on the table. "I can't shake the feeling that we're crossing a line. Are we sure this is the right thing to do?"

Naureen, sitting next to her, placed a reassuring hand on her arm. "We owe it to Zayd to find out the truth. If there's even a chance that the Wongs were involved, we can't just sit back and do nothing."

"Exactly," Danya affirmed, her voice gaining strength. "Zayd was more than just a mentor to us; he was family. His death can't be swept under the rug. If we have to step into the grey areas of morality to uncover the truth, then that's what we'll do."

Rami leaned back, arms crossed, his expression thoughtful. "But what happens if we find something? We need to be prepared for the consequences."

Danya nodded, grateful for the camaraderie and the sense of purpose that hung in the air. "That's why we need a plan. We'll meet tonight after hours at the funeral home. I've spoken to the director; he's agreed to let us in. We can conduct a thorough examination, and I'll lead the process."

Mira, always the voice of caution, raised her hand. "What about evidence collection? If we find anything, how do we ensure it's preserved?"

"We'll document everything meticulously," Danya said, her mind racing ahead to the planning. "Elodie, you'll handle the documentation—photos, notes, everything. Naureen and Kanchana, you'll assist with the medical equipment. Rami and Omar, you'll keep watch. We can't afford any interruptions."

Kanchana spoke up, her tone serious. "And let's not forget that we need to be respectful. Zayd deserves that. We're examining our own teacher, not just a body."

Danya met her gaze, appreciation swelling in her chest. "Absolutely. We'll approach this with the utmost respect and care. We're here to honour Zayd, not to exploit his death."

As the conversation flowed, a strategy began to crystallize. They would arrive at the funeral home well-prepared, their roles clear. Danya felt a flicker of hope amid the tension, knowing they were united in purpose.

"Alright, everyone," Danya said, glancing at her watch. "We need to gear up. It's almost time to leave." As they gathered their supplies, a sense of camaraderie enveloped them, a reminder of their shared history. Each of them had faced challenges and heartbreaks, but together, they had always emerged stronger.

The group made their way to the funeral home, the night air cool against their skin. Danya took a deep breath, steeling herself for what lay ahead. Each step felt heavy with the weight of their mission. Zayd's face flashed in her mind—his infectious smile, his laughter, the warmth of his mentorship. It felt surreal that they were about to explore the final chapter of his life.

When they arrived, the funeral home was eerily quiet, the kind of silence that wraps around you and chills you to the bone. Danya led them through the front doors, her heart pounding. The director greeted them with a nod, his expression serious but understanding. He knew their intent, and he respected their desire for answers.

"Just follow me," he said, leading them to a small examination room at the back. The dim lighting cast a sombre glow over the sterile environment, making it feel almost clinical. A gurney stood in the centre, draped with a white sheet, an ominous reminder of the reality they faced.

As the director left them to their task, Danya turned to her team. "Alright, let's do this. We owe it to Zayd."

They gathered around the gurney, the moment feeling surreal. Danya reached for the sheet, her hands trembling slightly. "On three. One... two... three."

With a swift motion, she pulled back the sheet, revealing Zayd's lifeless body. A heavy silence fell over the room. Danya's heart ached as she took in the sight of her friend, so still and silent.

"This is for you, Zayd," she whispered, a lump forming in her throat. She felt the eyes of her friends on her, sharing in her grief, but also her determination.

Mira stepped forward, the medical tools clutched tightly in her hands. "Let's start with a visual examination. We need to look for anything unusual—bruises, marks, anything that stands out."

Danya nodded, her mind focused. "Let's divide our tasks. I'll handle the examination, and Elodie, I'll need you to document everything I find."

As Danya carefully inspected Zayd's body, she felt a mixture of sorrow and resolve. Every bruise, every scar was a story waiting to be told. She worked methodically, searching for anything that could explain his untimely death.

Kanchana stood beside her, her expression solemn. "Do you think we'll find anything?"

"I don't know," Danya replied, her voice barely above a whisper. "But we have to try. If the Wongs are involved, we need to know how far their reach goes."

The minutes turned into what felt like hours as they meticulously documented their findings. Danya's hands trembled as she examined a small bruise on Zayd's wrist, one that hadn't been there during his last days. "This wasn't here before," she said, her voice breaking slightly. "I can't help but wonder..."

"What?" Naureen asked, her eyes widening.

"It looks like it could be a restraint mark," Danya said, her heart racing. "It doesn't make sense otherwise."

The gravity of the implication settled heavily on them. "What does this mean?" Mira asked, her voice trembling with disbelief.

"I don't know yet," Danya admitted, shaking her head. "But we need to keep searching."

They continued their examination, each discovery deepening their concern. When Elodie captured a photo of a small cut on Zayd's side, Danya felt a wave of nausea wash over her. "What happened to you, Zayd?" she murmured, brushing her fingers against the wound as if she could somehow unlock its secrets.

As they moved through the examination, Danya couldn't shake the feeling that they were walking a tightrope, balancing between honour and betrayal. Every step felt like a descent into darkness, but she was determined to press on.

Finally, they gathered their findings, each note a testament to their commitment to Zayd's memory. "We need to compile this evidence carefully," Danya said, her voice steadier now. "If we have enough to make a case, we can approach the authorities."

"Do you really think they'll listen?" Rami asked, scepticism colouring his tone.

"If we present our findings clearly and rationally, they have to," Danya replied, determination filling her voice. "But first, we need to get out of here without being caught."

As they prepared to leave, a sense of urgency took hold. They quickly packed up their equipment, adrenaline surging as they realized how close they had come to uncovering something profound. They were stepping into a world of darkness, but they were ready to confront it head-on.

With the evidence secured, they moved quietly through the funeral home, each of them aware that their actions could have far-reaching consequences. The weight of their mission pressed down on them, but they knew they were doing it for Zayd, for his legacy, and for the truth.

Once outside, the cool night air enveloped them, a stark contrast to the oppressive atmosphere they had just left behind. Danya glanced at her friends, their faces lit with a mix of determination and anxiety.

"We did it," she said, a small smile breaking through the tension. "We took the first step toward uncovering the truth."

Naureen took a deep breath, her eyes shining. "We owe it to Zayd to keep fighting."

As they walked away from the funeral home, Danya felt a sense of solidarity among them. They were no longer just friends—they were a team bound by purpose, ready to face whatever came next. With Zayd's spirit guiding them, they were prepared to unearth the echoes of deception that lingered in the shadows.

Danya's Diary

I can't sleep. The night air feels thick, like it's suffocating me, or maybe it's the weight of what we just did. I don't know how to put this into words, but I have to try. Maybe writing will help me make sense of everything, or at least help me remember why we did what we did.

Tonight, we examined Zayd. I never imagined I'd write those words. I never thought I'd be looking at his lifeless body, searching for clues about what killed him. It feels wrong, like I betrayed him somehow, even though I know it's the only way to find out the truth. It's not supposed to be like this. Friends shouldn't have to do this. Friends shouldn't have to wonder if someone they trusted was murdered.

But here I am. And here we are.

I still see his face, that damn white sheet. It's burned into my mind now. I keep telling myself that it was necessary, that we owed it to him to look, to find whatever answers we could. But there's a part of me that wishes we hadn't done it. Because now I have more questions than I did before. And I'm not sure I'm ready for the answers.

That mark on his wrist—I can't stop thinking about it. It wasn't there before. I know it wasn't. Could it really be a restraint mark? The thought makes my stomach churn. Was he tied down? Who would do that to him? He was gentle, he was kind. Zayd didn't have enemies. He didn't deserve this.

The cut we found, too—it's not deep, but it's enough. Enough to make me wonder what happened in those final moments. The authorities say it was natural causes, a sudden illness, but how can they explain that? They won't look deeper unless we make them. But are we ready for that? Are *we* even sure of what we found?

And then there's the others. I saw it in their eyes tonight. The same fear, the same doubts I'm carrying. They're brave—they came with me, they faced it with me, but are they all in this for the long haul? I need them to be. I can't do this alone. Not this time. Not when the stakes are so high.

There's no turning back now. We've already crossed a line, and I'm not sure how far we'll have to go before this is over. How much further can I push them, or myself? But we *have* to keep going. We owe that to Zayd. I owe him everything.

I keep thinking about what Naureen said before we started, about how we have to be respectful. She was right, of course. I could see how hard this was for her, for all of them. But I can't help but feel like respect wasn't enough. We're tampering with something bigger than us. Something we might not even fully understand yet.

Zayd's life was a puzzle, and his death is an even bigger one. It feels like every piece we find makes the picture darker, more twisted. The Wongs—how much do they really know? And why do I feel like this entire town is watching us, waiting for us to fail?

I keep going back to that moment when I touched Zayd's wrist, tracing the bruise with my fingers. My mind was racing, but my heart was frozen. It was like touching the truth for the first time, but the truth was cold and lifeless. I don't want that to be my last memory of him. I don't want him to become this case, this mission. But I don't know how to separate them anymore.

I wonder if we'll find justice, or if this will lead us down a darker path, one we can't come back from. But then I remember Zayd's laugh, his patience when he taught me how to handle the toughest situations in med school. He always believed in the good in people. That's why I have to keep pushing, even when everything feels impossible. I need to believe that uncovering the truth will honour him, somehow.

I'm scared, though. I haven't admitted that to anyone, not yet, but I'm scared. Not of what we'll find, but of how far we'll have to go to get there. How much will it cost us?

Maybe tomorrow will bring clarity. Maybe when we look over the evidence again, something will click into place, and it will all make sense. Maybe we'll finally have something we can take to the authorities.

Maybe. But for now, I can't shake this feeling that we're only scratching the surface. Something deeper is waiting to be uncovered, and when we do, it's going to change everything. I just hope we're ready for it.

But I'll say it again, just to remind myself: we owe this to Zayd. We owe him the truth, no Matter what. And I won't stop until we find it.

- Danya

Chapter 5: Bound to Delhi

Danya settled into her plush seat on the upper deck of the A380, the quiet hum of the engines soothing her nerves as she glanced over at her husband, who gave her hand a reassuring squeeze. Their children were already tucked into the window seats, eyes wide with excitement at the personal TVs and spacious surroundings. In the row ahead, Mira and Naureen had taken their places, Mira already engrossed in adjusting her seat controls and Naureen flipping through a magazine with a calm, collected air.

As the plane lifted off, Danya couldn't shake the anticipation swirling inside her. They were finally moving forward, taking this trip that she'd hoped would give them more clarity—and hopefully, answers. The cabin was calm, dimmed lights casting a warm, gentle glow as they flew through the night. After a while, Danya caught Mira's eye in front of her, nodding slightly toward the onboard lounge. Mira nudged Naureen, and the three of them quietly slipped away from their seats, heading toward the lounge at the rear of the business class cabin.

Once they reached the lounge, the comfortable, rounded space invited them to settle in, plush seating arranged around a low table. It wasn't long before Mira pulled out her tablet, connecting for a quick video call. Moments later, familiar faces flickered onto the screen—Elodie, Samira, Rami, Omar, Sara, Kanchana, and Laila, each offering Danya warm but curious looks as they appeared.

Danya glanced around at Mira and Naureen, their faces reflecting the same mix of determination and apprehension she felt. It was Naureen who broke the silence.

"All right, so let's go over the essentials. Mira and Kanchana, you'll be handling the nasoendoscope. We need to make sure the nasal passages are clear, and any inflammation or anomalies in that area are documented."

"Right," Mira replied, nodding. "We'll go slow and record each step carefully."

"Elodie, Samira, and Sara," Danya continued, turning toward their images on the screen, "you're our laryngoscopy team. Samira, it'll be critical to get a clear view of the vocal cords—Zayd's were a main concern, after all. Keep in mind any irregularities that might stand out to you, things that didn't appear in his earlier files."

Samira nodded, her face set. "Understood. We'll take it one step at a time, and each detail will be checked thoroughly."

Danya turned to Naureen. "As for us, pharynx is our focus, looking specifically for any signs around the laryngeal area that might have worsened things. The otoscope and tongue depressor should help us look deeper into what might have been missed."

"We'll stay as objective as possible," Naureen added, her eyes meeting Danya's with a firm resolve. "Every detail counts."

Kanchana chimed in from her end, "I'll make sure all nasoendoscope findings are clean and documented. We'll be vigilant, Danya."

They wrapped up the final details of their testing assignments, and everyone fell quiet for a moment, letting the weight of the tasks ahead settle over them. Just as Danya was about to end the call, Molly and Paula, 2 of her close friends who were radiologists, confidently through the ordeal, Joined. He greeted each of them warmly, immediately infusing the call with a sense of camaraderie.

"So," Molly began with a knowing look, "are we all prepared for the next steps?"

Danya smiled, nodding. "Ready as we can be. It feels good to have everyone's support on this. But" she added, "we're staying cautious, careful with each process."

They all murmured in agreement, and as the call ended, the heaviness lifted slightly, replaced by a shared sense of purpose. Danya leaned back, letting out a long breath. There was still a way to go, but at that moment, in the lounge high above the clouds, she felt a quiet confidence that they were on the right track.

Danya's Diary

I can't seem to shake this feeling. Sitting here on this plane, with the luxury of a lie-flat bed and the privacy of a door, I should feel relaxed. But I don't. Instead, there's this gnawing sense of anticipation inside me—an unease that keeps my thoughts racing. The seat is comfortable enough, and the hum of the engines provides a kind of dull background noise, but it doesn't drown out my mind.

We're flying over some distant part of the world, halfway to India. My husband and the kids are asleep, blissfully unaware of the whirlwind in my head. I look at them, peaceful in their sleep, and I feel... disconnected. As if I'm here, but not really here. It's as if I'm floating somewhere outside of myself, watching everything unfold from a distance. The more I try to ground myself in this moment, the further away I feel.

My husband's noticed, of course. He always does. He asked me earlier if I was all right if I needed anything. I told him I was fine. I smiled, too—because that's what you do, right? You smile so no one worries, so everything seems normal, even when it's not. But I know he sees through it. I saw the way he looked at me, his eyes searching mine, probably wondering what's really going on in my head.

What could I say? That I'm feeling overwhelmed by the sheer weight of what lies ahead? That I'm haunted by what we're trying to uncover? That the thought of Zayd still lingers in my mind like a shadow, refusing to fade?

No. I can't say any of that.

So I did what I always do—I brushed it off. Told him I was tired, that it's just the long flight, that I'll feel better once we land. He accepted it, but I know he's still worried. He's always there for me, always patient. But I don't want to burden him with this. I don't want to burden anyone with this. This isn't his Journey; it's mine.

I keep thinking about what I'll say when I see my family. It's been a while since I've visited them, and while they know the general reason for this trip, they don't know the whole truth. I haven't told them everything that's been happening, everything that's been unravelling. How could I?

What would they think if they knew the truth? About the plan? About what we're trying to find out? Would they understand? Would they think I'm losing my mind? Or worse, would they try to talk me out of it?

Sometimes I wonder if I'm being reckless. If this whole investigation is some elaborate form of denial—an excuse to avoid fully accepting that Zayd is gone. That he's really gone. It's been months since the funeral, and yet, it still doesn't feel real. How do you move on when there are so many unanswered questions? How do you find peace when every instinct is screaming that something isn't right?

I know I'm not alone in this. Laila, Kanchana, Elodie—they've all felt it too. We've all been circling around this same unease, this same sense that there's more to the story. But the further we go, the more isolated I feel. Everyone else seems to have their own ways of coping, their own ways of pushing through the grief. But me? I can't seem to shake it. The questions, the doubts—they're always there, always lingering.

I thought maybe this trip would give me some clarity. Maybe being away from everything for a little while would help me see things differently. But now that we're in the air, I'm not so sure. Instead, I feel more tangled up than ever. I feel like I'm carrying this invisible weight with me, this burden that no one else can see.

And yet, I know I have to keep going. I can't turn back now. Not when we're so close. Not when we might finally find the answers we've been looking for. But the fear... the fear is always there, lurking in the background. What if we're wrong? What if we find nothing? Or worse—what if we find something we're not prepared for?

I keep replaying the last few weeks in my head. The late-night meetings, the whispered conversations, the equipment handovers. The way Kanchana looked at me when she first agreed to help. The way Laila's voice trembled when she gave her blessing. The way Samira and Sara's eyes darkened when they realized what we were about to do. It's all so heavy. So much to carry.

Sometimes I wonder what Zayd would think if he knew what we were planning. Would he be proud of us for seeking the truth? Or would he tell us to stop, to let it go, to move on with our lives? I'll never know. That's the hardest part, I think—never knowing.

The lights in the cabin are dimmed now. Most of the other passengers are asleep. I'm the only one still awake, my thoughts buzzing like static, making it impossible to rest. I wish I could sleep. I wish I could close my eyes and drift into some peaceful oblivion, just for a little while. But every time I try, my mind pulls me back. Back to the funeral. Back to the questions. Back to the Wongs.

God, I hate even thinking their names. Alex and Anya Wong. The way they showed up at the funeral, the way they smirked, the way they looked at us as if we were nothing. It still makes my blood boil. They were so smug, so confident in their cruelty. And that's what terrifies me the most—that they know something we don't. That they're playing some game we haven't even figured out yet.

I keep telling myself that this trip is about more than just the investigation. That it's about reconnecting with family, about taking a break from the madness. But I can't help but feel like I'm running toward something, rather than away. Like this trip is just another step on this path I've been walking for too long now, a path I'm not sure I even chose.

I don't know what the next few days will bring. I don't know if I'll find any clarity, any answers. But I do know one thing: I can't keep living like this. I can't keep letting the shadows of the past control me, weigh me down. Something has to give.

For now, though, all I can do is wait. Wait for the plane to land. Wait to see my family, especially my parents. Wait for the next chapter to unfold, whatever it may be.

And hope—desperately hope—that we're not too late to find the truth.

Chapter 6: Into the Unknown

As Danya settled into her new seat aboard the second leg of their Journey on the 777, the hum of the engines reminded her of the purpose that lay ahead. This plane wasn't as spacious as the A380, but their seats were comfortable, offering the privacy and quiet they needed. Her husband had fallen asleep beside her, but her children, still sitting by the windows, were captivated by the view of the night sky above Dubai as the plane taxied for take-off.

In front of her, Mira and Naureen exchanged brief glances before Mira turned, giving Danya a small nod. There was a silent understanding between them now, a mutual determination that had only deepened over the hours. They were all restless to arrive in Delhi, to begin the examinations, and to find the answers they so desperately needed.

As the plane levelled off, Danya took out her tablet, connecting again with their team back home. She glanced toward Mira and Naureen, who leaned back to Join her conversation with the others on video. Familiar faces reappeared on the screen—Elodie, Samira, Rami, Omar, Sara, Kanchana, and Laila—all wearing expressions of both encouragement and concern.

"Let's talk preparations," Danya began, her voice barely above a whisper as she went over the next steps with her team.

Rami was the first to respond. "We've secured the necessary approvals for our process. We're all set to begin, and we'll be ready to assist with any additional data you might find on your end."

Danya nodded. "Excellent. Once we're there, Naureen and I will start with the pharynx assessments—otoscope and tongue depressor in hand. We'll look carefully for any signs we might have missed previously, anything that could point us in a different direction."

Naureen leaned in slightly. "We'll need to be vigilant, especially near the laryngeal area, and document everything thoroughly. No assumptions—just observations."

"Agreed," Elodie replied from her end, her face calm but focused. "Samira, Sara, and I will manage the laryngoscopy on this end, coordinating with you as we go."

Samira nodded thoughtfully. "Any irregularities we spot will go straight into the documentation. We want to be certain that we've covered every angle."

Beside her, Sara gave a firm nod. "Our priority is transparency and accuracy. If we find any signs that add up, we'll share it in real-time."

Kanchana and Mira chimed in next, outlining their plans for the nasoendoscope assessments. Kanchana's voice was steady as she spoke, a calm presence in the mix. "Each section will be recorded, Danya. We'll move carefully through each stage and compare notes to make sure everything aligns."

Danya could feel the weight of their unified commitment, a collective push to find answers that could explain what had happened to Zayd, answers that had eluded them up to this point.

They continued to discuss the planning and preparations, pausing only when the plane hit a slight pocket of turbulence. Molly and Paula Joined the call toward the end, his familiar voice adding a layer of reassurance.

"So, everyone set for the next phase?" he asked, his tone friendly yet perceptive. "You're all handling this with more dedication than I can imagine."

Danya exchanged glances with Mira and Naureen, a sense of gratitude filling her. "We're set, girls. Knowing you're all with us makes this manageable."

The rest of the team nodded, offering smiles and words of encouragement as the call ended. Afterward, Danya leaned back into her seat, exhaling slowly. The weight of the task ahead was still heavy, but with every mile closer to Delhi, she felt more certain of their purpose.

Danya's Diary

It's late, somewhere over the Arabian Sea. I'm not sure how long we've been in the air, but my mind feels as restless as the hum of the engines around me. I feel the quietness next to me where my husband and the kids are sound asleep, but there's this pull, this ache for answers I can't shake. I keep replaying our last few days in my head, the endless discussions, the preparation, the farewells to everyone back home who couldn't make this trip with us. And the turbulence of emotions under it all.

Today started with a strange mix of excitement and anticipation as we boarded the first plane. It's been a while since I last travelled with all of them—Mira, Naureen, my family—and something about it felt surreal. Watching the kids marvel at the space around them, laughing over the small luxuries of our seats and the privacy it brought, it felt like a brief escape from all that's happened. But even then, the reality of what we're setting out to do pulled me back.

Sitting here, with Naureen and Mira in the row in front of us, I keep circling back to the conversation we had in the onboard lounge during the first flight. I remember looking around that space—quiet, dimly lit, with only a few other passengers around—and feeling the pressure of the moment. There we were, somewhere between continents, discussing procedures and plans in the intimacy of an airplane lounge. And yet, despite the oddness of it all, there was a clarity to that conversation I didn't expect.

Naureen and Mira sat across from me, their expressions intense but open. Naureen leaned in, hands wrapped around her cup as if anchoring herself, while Mira kept glancing out the window, visibly nervous but steeling herself for the task. We talked through each step, and it hit me, as it always does at moments like these, how much I trust these people. Naureen will be focused on the pharynx, Mira on the nasoendoscope. Kanchana and Elodie will Join us remotely, each person offering their skill set, as meticulous and careful as possible.

But even as we discussed the tests, the terms felt technical, mechanical. Our words—otoscope, laryngoscopy, pharynx, tongue depressor—felt like Armor, protecting us from the rawness Beneath it all.

When I looked down at my tablet, there was the familiar group staring back at me through the screen: Kanchana, Elodie, Samira, Rami, Omar, Sara, Laila—all the people who have become part of this mission we never intended to take on. We laid out everything in sequence, the steps, each of us confirming our tasks like pieces of a puzzle locking into place.

Naureen and I will examine the pharynx, combing through each detail for anomalies. Meanwhile, Kanchana and Mira will be responsible for the nasoendoscope, their precise work as essential as the air we breathe. Then there's Samira, Sara, and Elodie on laryngoscopy, their eyes peeled for any unusual signs that could alter the course of everything we know.

There's something surreal about strategizing like this, about planning out every little step as if we're gearing up for a campaign. And I guess, in a way, we are. We're taking on something I never imagined I'd have the courage to confront, determined to uncover the truth in Zayd's passing.

We had a brief moment with Molly and Paula on the call, too, who brought with him a sense of calm that only he can seem to manage in situations like these. His words, his smile, his quiet encouragement reminded me of why we're doing this. It's easy to lose sight of it amidst the whirlwind of terms, charts, and instruments, but Molly and Paula's support brought me back to that foundation. We need the truth. For Zayd, for ourselves, for everyone else whose lives have been turned upside down.

I remember ending the call with a renewed sense of focus, but even after we'd gone back to our seats, the feeling lingered. Mira, Naureen, and I exchanged a glance before settling back in. We didn't have to say anything; the understanding was there, hanging in the air between us. We're in this together.

Now, back on this second plane, the atmosphere feels different. Less chatter, less laughter, just quiet determination. Naureen is resting, Mira seems to be doing some mental run-through of her tasks, and I find myself unable to close my eyes, my mind racing through every possibility of what we'll find—or what we won't.

Zayd's memory feels alive with every mile, pushing us closer to a place I'm not sure I'm fully prepared for, but one I know we must face. I think of him often, moments flashing like old photographs—his laugh, his fierce intelligence, his loyalty. It's those things that keep me grounded, even now, up here in this quiet, endless stretch of sky.

We'll be landing soon, and I know that every second from that point on will Matter.

Chapter 7: Family Ties

As the plane descended toward Delhi, Danya felt the familiar mixture of excitement and apprehension swirling within her. The last few hours had passed in a blur, filled with fleeting conversations and half-hearted attempts to rest. Now, as the landscape outside the window began to take shape, she caught sight of the sprawling city below, dotted with temples, vibrant markets, and the glistening coastline that marked the southern edge of India.

"Mummy, look! There's the ocean!" her daughter exclaimed from her window seat, eyes wide with wonder.

"Isn't it beautiful?" Danya replied, a soft smile breaking through her apprehension. She turned to her husband, who sat beside her, his hand resting on her knee in a comforting gesture. They had been through so much together, and now they were on the brink of something monumental.

The flight attendants began their final preparations for landing, and Danya's thoughts drifted to her family awaiting them at the airport. Her parents had made the trip from their small town, excited and nervous to see their daughter and her children after so long. Danya's heart swelled with emotion at the thought of the reunion. She hadn't seen them in over a year, not since the funeral. Their absence had left a gaping hole in her life, but now they were coming together for a cause that felt both noble and daunting.

Once the plane touched down, Danya felt a rush of adrenaline. After disembarking, they made their way through the airport, the bustling crowds reminding her of the vibrant energy of India. Her heart raced as they exited the terminal, and she scanned the sea of faces, her eyes finally landing on her parents.

"Mom! Dad!" she shouted, breaking into a sprint toward them. Danya's mother, Asha, looked radiant despite the years that had added fine lines to her face. Her father, Ramesh, stood beside her, his presence a source of steadfast support. As Danya reached them, they enveloped her in a tight embrace, the kind that felt like coming home.

"Oh, Danya! We've missed you so much!" Asha exclaimed, pulling back to look at her daughter. Her eyes were shimmering with tears. "And the children! Where are they?"

"Right here, Nani!" her son piped up, racing over to his grandmother, who scooped him into her arms.

Ramesh chuckled, glancing at Danya's husband. "Good to see you, son. You've taken good care of my daughter, I see." His tone was teasing but warm, and Danya could see the fondness in her father's eyes.

"Of course, Uncle. It's my duty," he replied, smiling back.

Danya stepped back, taking a moment to collect her thoughts. She felt the weight of what lay ahead—both the joy of the reunion and the difficult conversation that awaited her. "I'm so glad you're here. There's so much to tell you."

Just then, she spotted her brother, Ravi, walking toward them with his younger siblings in tow—Arjun, her other brother, and little Meera, her younger sister. Ravi, tall and broad-shouldered, held his siblings close. The sight of him stirred a deep sense of comfort within Danya, but it was also laced with sadness at the reason they had gathered.

"Danya! You made it!" Ravi called out, rushing to her and pulling her into a strong embrace. "I can't believe it's been so long."

"I know," Danya said, her voice wavering slightly. "It's been too long."

Arjun joined in next, a cheeky grin on his face. "I thought you'd forgotten about us! Did you think you could just leave us for a year?"

Meera, who had always looked up to Danya, bounced up to her, her dark eyes shining. "Didi, you look different! You've grown taller, right?"

Danya chuckled, ruffling her sister's hair. "It's just the shoes, I promise. But it's so good to see all of you."

As they all settled into a group, the warmth of family surrounded Danya, but she couldn't shake the urgency of their mission. After some time exchanging pleasantries and catching up on family news, she finally cleared her throat, her heart racing.

"Can we sit down somewhere quieter?" she suggested, her voice steady despite the chaos of emotions swirling within her. "There's something important I need to share."

"Sure, there's a café just outside the airport," Ravi offered, his expression turning serious. "Let's go there."

As they made their way to the café, Danya felt a mixture of dread and relief wash over her. It was vital that they understood the gravity of the situation, and she knew her family would want to support her. But how could she convey the magnitude of their investigation without overwhelming them?

Once they were settled at a round table in the café, the aroma of freshly brewed coffee and spiced snacks filled the air. Danya took a deep breath, gathering her thoughts.

"I'm so glad we're all together again, but I need to talk to you about something that's been weighing heavily on me since... since Zayd passed," she started, her voice slightly trembling.

Asha reached across the table, her hand resting gently on Danya's. "You can tell us anything, dear. We're here for you."

Danya swallowed hard, trying to suppress the knot forming in her throat. "The thing is his death... it didn't feel right to me. There were so many questions left unanswered, and I couldn't just let it go. I've been working with some friends to look into it further."

Ravi furrowed his brow. "What do you mean? You think it was something more than just cancer?"

"Yes, that's exactly it," Danya replied, her heart racing. "We're investigating. We want to find out if there was anything suspicious—any signs that suggest foul play. I know it sounds crazy, but there are just too many coincidences."

A silence fell over the table as her siblings and parents processed her words. Arjun looked concerned, glancing at Ravi. "What kind of investigation are you talking about?"

"Mom, Dad, I know this is hard to hear," Danya said, her voice growing steadier. "But we're planning to conduct a series of examinations on Zayd's remains, looking for any signs that might indicate he was poisoned or harmed in any way. I can't shake the feeling that something isn't right, and I need your support."

Ramesh's brows knitted together, and Asha's eyes widened in disbelief. "Are you sure you want to do this, Danya? It feels... risky. What if you find something for which you aren't prepared?"

"I know it sounds daunting, but I feel like it's the only way to honour him," Danya insisted. "Zayd was a good man who deserved to have his truth known. And I can't just let this go."

Ravi leaned forward, his expression serious. "What exactly do you need from us? We're here for you, no Matter what."

Danya's heart swelled at her brother's words. "I just need your understanding and support. We've all been affected by this tragedy, and I think together we can uncover the truth. You don't have to be directly involved, but I want you to know what's happening."

"I'll help in any way I can," Arjun said, nodding. "Just tell me what you need."

Meera, who had been listening intently, spoke up. "Didi, I want to help too! Whatever you need, I'll do it."

Asha squeezed Danya's hand, her voice steady but filled with concern. "As long as you're careful, I'll support whatever decision you make. Your happiness and peace of mind are what Matters most to me."

Danya felt a wave of gratitude wash over her. "Thank you, Mom. It means the world to me."

As they continued to discuss the situation, Danya noticed the way her family rallied around her, offering encouragement and understanding. She felt a sense of relief wash over her. The burden of secrecy had been lifted, and she no longer felt alone in her quest for answers.

"We can also reach out to our family friends, the doctors, and anyone who can provide insights into Zayd's condition," Ravi suggested. "The more information we gather, the better prepared we'll be for whatever comes next."

"Exactly," Danya replied, feeling more hopeful. "We need to cover all bases."

They spent the next hour discussing planning and brainstorming ideas, all while sipping on sweet chai and snacking on crispy dosas. Laughter intermingled with serious conversation, a blend of Joy and sorrow that felt both comforting and painful.

Eventually, as the sun began to set, casting a warm golden hue over the café, Danya looked around at her family, her heart swelling with appreciation. "Thank you all for being here. I know it's not easy, but I believe we can get through this together."

As they prepared to leave, Danya felt a renewed sense of purpose. The Journey ahead would be fraught with challenges, but she was determined to seek the truth for Zayd—and for herself. Family bonds, she realized, were not just about shared blood; they were about shared struggles, shared pain, and ultimately, shared love.

Danya's Diary

Today, I find myself overwhelmed by a wave of emotions that are difficult to articulate. As I sit here in this quiet corner of our temporary home in Delhi, the echoes of laughter and the warmth of my family surround me, yet I feel a deep sense of melancholy that seems to linger just Beneath the surface. My heart aches for Zayd, for the loss that has reshaped my entire world. It's strange how grief can morph over time—from an initial shock into a dull throb that never really goes away.

The trip here was both exhilarating and exhausting. I watched my children's faces light up as we took off, their excitement palpable. They peered out the window at the clouds, imagining all sorts of adventures in the sky. Yet amidst their Joy, I felt a familiar knot tighten in my stomach, a reminder of the heavy burden I carry.

It was a bittersweet moment, one that encapsulated the duality of my existence right now: happiness and sorrow entwined, forever in conflict. The flight from Dubai to Delhi on the A380 was a blur of activity—navigating the crowds, comforting my kids during turbulence, and trying to stifle my own anxieties about our mission. Even though the airline provided every luxury, with spacious seats and an onboard lounge, I couldn't quite enjoy it the way I wanted. My mind was too preoccupied with thoughts of what lay ahead.

Upon landing, the chaos of Delhi's airport engulfed me. The air was thick with humidity, and the sounds of honking horns and excited chatter filled my ears. But amidst the bustling crowds, there was an undeniable warmth in the air that seemed to reach out and wrap around me. I felt the familiar pulse of home, even though I knew it was different now. Everything was tinged with a sense of urgency, as if the city itself understood why we were here.

Reuniting with my parents, Asha and Ramesh, was a floodgate of emotions. Seeing their faces, filled with love and worry, brought tears to my eyes. My mother enveloped me in her arms, her familiar scent of jasmine and coconut oil bringing back memories of my childhood. I missed this connection, this deep-rooted bond that anchored me to my past. I felt a sense of comfort wash over me as my children jumped into their grandparents' arms, their laughter mixing with the Joyful chaos of our reunion.

After the initial rush of emotions settled, I knew I had to talk to my family about why we were really here. Gathering everyone at the café just outside the airport was a challenge. I could see the concern etched on their faces, the way they leaned in closer as I revealed the truth about Zayd's death and the investigation that was unfolding. I felt like a tightrope walker, balancing my desire to honour Zayd's memory with the need to shield my family from further pain.

I could see my siblings processing the information, their brows furrowed with concern. Ravi was the first to voice his thoughts. "What do you mean, you think it was something more than just cancer?" His tone was filled with genuine confusion and concern, and it felt good to know he cared so deeply. I knew it wasn't just a wild theory in my head; there were signs that warranted further investigation.

As I spoke, I watched my parents' expressions shift from surprise to worry. Asha's voice trembled slightly when she said, "Are you sure you want to do this, Danya? It feels... risky. What if you find something for which you aren't prepared?" Her protective instinct was palpable, and I felt a mixture of guilt and gratitude for her concern.

I reassured her, my voice steady, "I can't let it go. Zayd deserves the truth, and so do I." I saw understanding slowly creep into her expression, and it filled me with a sense of hope. If my parents and siblings stood by my side, I believed we could face whatever lay ahead.

Arjun's willingness to help meant a lot, too. "Whatever you need, just tell me." His support felt like a lifeline, grounding me in the chaos of uncertainty. I could sense my family rallying around me, their solidarity fuelling my determination to seek justice for Zayd.

Despite the weight of our conversation, there were moments of levity, too. Meera, always the light-hearted one, chimed in with her usual enthusiasm, "Didi, I want to help too! Whatever you need, I'll do it." Her innocence made me smile amidst the seriousness of our mission.

Later, as we sipped chai and snacked on dosas, I couldn't help but reflect on how much had changed. Just last year, we had been gathered for Zayd's funeral, filled with sorrow and confusion. Now, we were here, united in purpose and love. I felt an overwhelming surge of gratitude for my family and the strength they provided. I knew they were going to help me shoulder the burden of this investigation, and it felt like a weight had been lifted from my shoulders.

After our heartfelt discussion, the mood lightened. We started sharing stories from the past, reminiscing about family gatherings and traditions. The laughter of my children, coupled with the warmth of my family, created a tapestry of love and support that I desperately needed. It reminded me that even in darkness, there could be light, and together, we could find a way through.

As the sun began to set, casting golden hues across the sky, I felt a renewed sense of hope and determination. I knew that the Journey ahead wouldn't be easy, but I had my family by my side, and that made all the difference.

Before we left the café, Ravi suggested we reach out to family friends in the medical community, and I wholeheartedly agreed. There were so many avenues we could explore, and having my family's input and connections would be invaluable.

I think back to our flight here, how it felt to soar above the clouds, a metaphor for the Journey I am about to embark on—navigating through uncertainty and striving for clarity. The conversations we had, filled with both trepidation and excitement, are etched in my memory. I feel buoyed by the support of my family, and for the first time in a while, I believe we might find the answers we're searching for.

In this strange mix of grief and hope, I'm reminded that family is everything. They are the foundation upon which I can build my quest for truth. I know the road ahead is fraught with challenges, but together, we will navigate it, step by step, until we uncover the truth behind Zayd's death.

And with that thought, I close my diary for now, taking a moment to breathe deeply and savour the love surrounding me. I am not alone in this, and that, more than anything, gives me the strength to continue.

Chapter 8: Unbroken Bonds

Danya found herself standing in the bustling arrivals hall of Indira Gandhi International Airport, surrounded by the familiar sights and sounds of her hometown. Delhi felt like a balm, a place where the complexities of her life fell away, if only temporarily. The air was tinged with the aromas of chai and street food, and the noise of conversations in Hindi and Telugu mixed in with the background din of the airport. Here, amid the chaos, was where she felt most at home.

She glanced at Nihal, her husband, who was helping their children gather their things. Despite the fatigue from the Journey, there was a glint of anticipation in his eyes, perhaps the same spark she felt—an eagerness to reconnect with family. Beside them stood Mira and Naureen, her longtime friends who had come along on this Journey for support and solidarity. The bond between them had grown even stronger through Zayd's death and the investigation that followed, and their presence made Danya feel less alone in the whirlwind that had become her life.

Finally, she spotted them: her parents, Asha and Ramesh, waving from across the hall. A rush of emotions surged within her as she took in her father's wide smile, her mother's eyes misty with unshed tears. Her elder brother, Ravi, was next to them, his arms crossed, a familiar expression of both relief and restrained excitement on his face. Standing close to him were her younger siblings—Arjun and Meera. Arjun, in his typical casual style, was grinning, while Meera bounced slightly on her toes, unable to hide her enthusiasm.

As Danya moved toward them, her children broke away and ran straight to their grandparents, who welcomed them with open arms. In that moment, Danya's heart swelled with a sense of belonging that no other place could provide. Here, in the arms of her family, the weight of recent events lifted, if only for a fleeting moment.

After a round of warm hugs and quiet exchanges, the group made their way out to the waiting cars. On the drive back to her family's home, Danya sat between her mother and father, with Nihal and the kids in the car behind them. Ravi had stayed back to finish a few things at the airport, promising to Join them later. The cityscape of Delhi passed by outside the window, and Danya found herself flooded with memories of growing up here. The years she spent playing in the narrow streets with her siblings, the scent of her mother's cooking wafting from the kitchen, the lazy summer evenings when they would sit on the rooftop and share stories—it all came rushing back.

When they arrived home, Danya felt a wave of nostalgia hit her. The familiar scent of sandalwood mixed with turmeric greeted her as she stepped inside, and she felt as though no time had passed at all. Her mother's home had always been a sanctuary, a place where all troubles seemed smaller and every corner held a cherished memory. The decor hadn't changed much over the years—the wooden idols of deities in the prayer room, the faded family photographs on the wall, and the worn, comfortable sofa in the living room. It was all just as she remembered.

Once everyone was settled, Danya felt the need to share the reason for their visit. She knew it would be difficult to relive the events surrounding Zayd's death and their ongoing investigation, but her family deserved to know. They sat together in the living room, the children in the playroom with her mother, while her father and siblings gathered around her. She took a deep breath, glancing at Nihal, who gave her a reassuring nod. Then, she began to speak.

"It's about Zayd," Danya said, her voice steady but tinged with sorrow. "We're looking into his death because... well, there are things that just don't add up. His illness, the way it progressed—it doesn't feel right." She paused, searching for the right words. "We think there might have been something else going on, something we missed."

Her father, Ramesh, leaned forward, concern etched into his face. "What do you mean, Danya? Are you saying it wasn't just the cancer?"

"We don't know for certain, but yes... I believe there could be more to it. Zayd was so close to Ravi. They were like brothers." Danya glanced at Ravi, who was staring intently at her, his face unreadable. "I couldn't let this go without trying to understand what really happened. Zayd deserves that."

Ravi sighed, rubbing the back of his neck, clearly troubled. "Zayd was one of us," he said, his voice thick with emotion. "We practically grew up together. If there's something wrong—if someone did this to him—we have to know."

Asha, who had been silent until now, placed a gentle hand on Danya's shoulder. "I understand, beta," she said softly, her eyes reflecting a mixture of grief and acceptance. "Zayd was family to all of us. If there's a chance you can find the truth, then you must do it."

Her younger brother, Arjun, nodded in agreement, his expression uncharacteristically serious. "And if you need any help from us, just say the word. We're here for you, Didi."

Danya felt a surge of gratitude for her family's support. Knowing they believed in her mission strengthened her resolve. She glanced at Nihal, whose reassuring gaze filled her with courage.

Ravi cleared his throat. "So, how do you plan to proceed with this investigation?" he asked, his tone practical.

"We'll start with some preliminary tests," Danya replied, her mind already beginning to focus on the steps ahead. "Basic examinations to see if anything unusual shows up. We have a few close friends back home who are willing to help with different assessments." She listed off the names and tests: "Naureen and I will handle the pharyngeal assessments. Kanchana and Mira are set to help with the nasoendoscope. Then Samira, Sara, and Elodie will assist with the laryngoscopy."

Ravi nodded, absorbing the information. "Sounds like you've thought this through," he said, a hint of pride in his voice.

The conversation shifted, touching on the planning of the investigation and the next steps they would take. As Danya spoke, she noticed her sister, Meera, looking at her with admiration, and she felt a renewed sense of purpose. For all the challenges that lay ahead, she knew she wasn't alone.

Later, after a dinner filled with laughter and stories, Danya found herself sitting with her father on the terrace. The city lights stretched out before them, casting a soft glow over the rooftops. The warm night air was filled with the sounds of distant honking and the occasional bark of a street dog.

Ramesh looked at her, his eyes wise and knowing. "You've taken on a big task, Danya," he said quietly. "Are you ready for this?"

She took a moment before answering. "I don't know if I'll ever be fully ready, Papa. But I have to do this. For Zayd. For Ravi. For all of us." She looked out over the city, feeling a deep sense of resolve settle within her. "I have to know what happened to him."

Her father placed a comforting hand on her shoulder. "You're stronger than you realize, beta. And we're with you every step of the way."

Danya leaned into his embrace, feeling a mixture of relief and determination. Whatever lay ahead, she knew she could face it—with her family's love and support guiding her through.

The next morning, they gathered in the living room once again. The kids were still asleep, and Asha was in the kitchen preparing breakfast. As Danya and her siblings talked, Ravi shared stories about Zayd, recounting moments that made them laugh and remember the kind-hearted man who had been a part of their lives.

"He was family, even if not by blood," Ravi said, his voice cracking slightly. "It's strange to think of him as gone. But I know he's with us, somehow."

Danya smiled, feeling a surge of warmth as she looked around at her family. The love they had for Zayd transcended the boundaries of biology, creating an unbreakable bond that tied them together.

As the day went on, they planned their next steps, discussing how they would approach the tests and whom they could rely on for support. Each member of her family played a role, and Danya felt an overwhelming sense of gratitude for the people surrounding her.

She knew the Journey ahead would be long and challenging, filled with unknowns. But she also knew that, with her family beside her, she could face whatever came her way.

Danya's Diary

I can hardly believe I'm back in Delhi, standing in my parents' house, surrounded by the familiar scents and sounds that shaped my childhood. The Journey here, from the heavy emotional weight of Zayd's loss to the warm embrace of family, has felt surreal, like living in two different worlds simultaneously. Each moment carries its own significance, a blend of grief and relief, the memories of our past intertwined with the heavy presence of our current reality.

When we landed at the airport, I was struck by the chaos of it all. The hustle and bustle of travellers, the cacophony of voices in a blend of languages, the fragrant street food wafting through the air—every detail washed over me like a comforting wave, reminding me of my roots. I had missed this place, the vibrancy of Delhi, even amidst the pain of why we were here.

Nihal, my husband, was a steady presence beside me, gently guiding our children through the arrival hall. Watching him interact with my parents filled my heart with warmth. They welcomed him with open arms, just as they did with our children. The love in that room was palpable, and it was a soothing balm against the raw wounds we were all carrying. Seeing my parents, Amma and Nana, was bittersweet; their smiles were bright, but their eyes held shadows of concern for what we were facing.

As we drove home, I gazed out the window, taking in the sights of the city I grew up in. The trees lining the streets, the familiar shops, the buzz of life outside—everything felt like a time capsule, transporting me back to my childhood. It was a mixture of nostalgia and a painful reminder of what we had lost.

Upon arriving at my parents' house, I was enveloped in memories. The sight of the old prayer room, the familiar aroma of Amma's cooking wafting from the kitchen—it all felt so comforting. The living room, adorned with family photographs, encapsulated years of love, Joy, and shared moments. I felt a wave of nostalgia wash over me, as if the walls themselves were whispering stories of our past.

Once we settled in, I realized I needed to share what was happening with my family. They deserved to know why we had come, why my heart was heavy. I gathered everyone in the living room, and as I spoke, I saw their faces shift from curiosity to concern.

"Zayd... he's gone," I said, the words tasting bitter on my tongue. "And we believe there's more to his death than just the illness." I could see the weight of the moment sink into my family. Their expressions were a mixture of sadness and understanding. They knew how close we had all been to Zayd.

Amma's hand found mine, squeezing gently, her eyes shimmering with tears. "What do you mean, beta?" she asked, her voice steady but filled with concern.

"There are questions, Amma. Things don't add up about his illness, the way it progressed so quickly. It's not just about the cancer anymore. I need to find out what really happened."

Nana, ever the pillar of strength, leaned forward, his brow furrowed in thought. "We'll help you, Danya. Whatever it takes. You're not alone in this."

I felt a swell of gratitude wash over me, mixed with the heartache of our loss. My siblings, Ravi, Arjun, and Meera, echoed their support. Ravi looked at me with a serious expression, his eyes reflecting the bond we shared, the responsibility we felt for Zayd's memory. "We'll figure this out together, Didi," he assured me.

The discussions continued long into the night, revolving around the next steps in our investigation. The logistical planning was daunting, but with my family at my side, I felt a renewed sense of strength. The plans we laid out were filled with determination, and every voice in the room was filled with conviction. I could see how much Zayd had meant to them, and it made me want to fight even harder for answers.

As the days passed, we spent time reminiscing about Zayd, sharing stories that made us laugh and cry. Each anecdote added layers to our understanding of who he had been—a man full of life, laughter, and love. Our conversations shifted seamlessly between the past and the present, binding us closer together, reminding us of our shared history and the ties that united us.

In quieter moments, I found myself reflecting on the significance of family. We often take for granted the support and love that surrounds us until faced with challenges that shake us to our core. The loss of Zayd, however painful, had brought us together in a way that I had never anticipated. It was a painful reminder that life can change in an instant, and we must cherish every moment, every connection.

One evening, while the children played in the background, I took a moment to step out onto the terrace. The night air was cool and refreshing, and I found myself gazing at the stars scattered across the vast sky. Each twinkle felt like a reminder of the countless memories shared and the love that connected us all, even across distances. I whispered a silent prayer for Zayd, hoping he could somehow feel the love surrounding him, wherever he was.

In those moments of solitude, I began to understand that this journey we were on was not just about uncovering the truth behind Zayd's death. It was also about healing, about coming together as a family to navigate the storm that life had thrown our way. The road ahead might be filled with uncertainties, but I knew I wouldn't have to walk it alone.

With each passing day, the determination to find answers only grew stronger. Conversations with my siblings turned into brainstorming sessions filled with ideas and strategies. We would discuss the assessments and tests, each plan etched in determination. The focus was on Zayd, but the process also brought us closer, reminding us of our shared commitment to one another.

I felt a sense of empowerment that I hadn't felt in a long time. Each discussion was a step forward, a way to honour Zayd's memory and legacy. I knew that whatever the outcome of our investigation, we would face it together, as a family bound by love and shared experiences.

As I write this, I can't help but feel a mixture of hope and sorrow. Hope for what lies ahead, and sorrow for the loss that brought us together in this way. But I'm reminded that in every ending, there is also a beginning, and I am ready to embrace whatever comes next, surrounded by the people I love most in this world.

Chapter 9: A Walk with Nana

The morning sunbathed Delhi in a warm, golden light, casting long shadows along the quiet streets near her childhood home. Danya stood at the edge of the garden, watching the small blooms sway gently in the breeze. The city was just waking up, and the faint hum of distant activity carried through the air. Her father, —or Nana, as she and her siblings had always called him—appeared at her side.

"Shall we go for a walk, beta?" he asked, his voice as steady and grounding as it had always been.

Danya nodded, slipping her arm through his. They set off together, moving past the wrought-iron gate and out onto the familiar streets.

The neighbourhood was a blend of old and new, much like her memories of it. The once-vivid walls of some homes were now weathered with age, while others bore the fresh marks of renovations. As they strolled past small shops, leafy trees, and the occasional chai vendor, the air seemed lighter, almost comforting.

"You've been quiet since last night," Nana began, his gaze fixed ahead as they walked. "I know this isn't easy for you."

Danya sighed, her steps slowing for a moment. "It's not, Nana. It feels like there's so much to do, and I don't even know where to begin. Zayd's death… it's not just grief. It's questions, doubts, and this overwhelming need to make things right."

Her father nodded, his face thoughtful. "You've always been like this, you know. Even as a child. Always searching for answers, always driven to fix things. Do you remember the time Ravi broke his cricket bat?"

Danya laughed softly at the memory. "He was devastated, wasn't he? And I spent hours trying to glue it back together, even though it was hopeless."

"Yes," Nana said with a small smile. "But you didn't give up. That's who you are, Danya. You don't give up, even when the odds are against you. Zayd would be proud of that."

The mention of Zayd brought a wave of emotion crashing over her. She blinked back tears and focused on the rhythmic sound of their footsteps.

"I just wish he were here, Nana. He was more than a brother to me—he was family in every sense of the word. Losing him feels like losing a part of myself."

Nana stopped walking and turned to face her, placing a hand gently on her shoulder. His eyes, warm and wise, searched hers.

"You're not alone in this, Danya," he said firmly. "You have Nihal, your children, your Amma, your siblings—and me. We're all here for you. And Zayd may not be here in person, but his spirit, his love, it's with you. Always."

Danya nodded, her throat tight with emotion. They resumed their walk, turning down a quieter street lined with old banyan trees.

"Nana," she began hesitantly, "do you think I'm doing the right thing? Pursuing this investigation? Digging into Zayd's death instead of just accepting it?"

Her father was silent for a moment, considering her question. Then he spoke, his voice steady and measured.

"I think that you're doing what your heart tells you is right. And that's all any of us can do. Zayd was a man of integrity; he valued truth more than anything else. If you believe that uncovering the truth about his death is what he would have wanted, then you're honouring him by doing this."

His words were a balm to her restless thoughts, grounding her in a way few things could. They walked on in comfortable silence for a while, passing a group of children playing cricket in a narrow alley. The sight brought a wistful smile to Danya's face.

"It's strange," she said after a while. "Being back here, seeing all of this. It's like nothing has changed, but at the same time, everything feels different."

"Life moves forward," Nana said simply. "Places stay the same, but we change. Our experiences shape how we see the world. That's why coming home feels both familiar and foreign. You're not the same person who left."

They reached a small park at the end of the street, where a few early risers were practicing yoga on the grass. Nana guided her to a Bench under a sprawling neem tree, and they sat down, watching the scene unfold before them.

"Do you miss it here, Danya?" he asked after a while.

"Sometimes," she admitted. "I miss the simplicity of it. The closeness of family. Life feels different now—busier, more complicated. But I also love the life Nihal and I have built. The kids, our home… it's just that right now, everything feels so uncertain."

Nana reached over and took her hand in his, his grip reassuring.

"Uncertainty is a part of life, beta. But so is resilience. You've faced challenges before, and you've come out stronger each time. This is no different. You have the strength to see this through."

Danya leaned her head against his shoulder, feeling a sense of peace settle over her. For the first time in days, the weight on her chest felt a little lighter.

"Thank you, Nana," she said softly.

"For what?" he asked, his tone light and teasing.

"For being you," she replied with a smile. "For always knowing what to say, and for reminding me of who I am."

They sat in companionable silence for a while longer, watching the world go by. The morning sun climbed higher, casting dappled shadows through the branches above them. Danya knew there was still a long road ahead, but in that moment, with her father by her side, she felt ready to face it.

When they finally stood to leave, the city seemed a little less daunting, and her steps felt a little lighter. Nana's words stayed with her, a quiet reminder of the strength she carried within.

Danya's Diary

There's something comforting about walking with Nana. It's not just the rhythm of our steps or the familiar streets of Delhi; it's the steady presence he brings, like an anchor in a storm. He doesn't need to say much, but when he does, his words stay with me, carving little pockets of peace into the chaos of my thoughts.

This morning, we walked through the neighbourhood I grew up in. I hadn't realized how much I missed it until I was back. The streets lined with banyan trees, the small shops with their chipping paint, the faint smell of spices wafting from someone's kitchen—it all feels like a time capsule, untouched by the whirlwind of years. But Nana reminded me, as he always does, that it's not the places that change. It's us.

"You've grown, Danya," he said quietly as we walked. "Not just in years, but in how you carry yourself. I see it."

I couldn't help but smile at that. Nana has a way of noticing things about me that even I overlook. For so long, I've been consumed by the demands of life—being a wife, a mother, a sister, and now, someone seeking answers to questions I never thought I'd have to ask. To hear that he sees me, really sees me, feels like a small gift.

We talked about Zayd for a while. Nana told me how much Zayd reminded him of Ravi when we were younger. "The way he protects you," Nana said, his voice tinged with a kind of wistful pride. "It's like looking at Ravi all over again."

I had never made that connection before, but now it seems so obvious. Zayd and Ravi share the same quiet strength, the same unyielding loyalty. Perhaps that's why I've always felt such a kinship with Zayd, why his loss felt so personal.

As we turned a corner, Nana paused and looked at the sunlight filtering through the leaves. "Danya," he began, "you have a way of holding everything together for everyone else. But who holds you together?"

The question caught me off guard. I didn't have an answer for him. I've been so focused on being the glue for my family that I've forgotten what it means to be cared for in return.

Nana reached out and placed a hand on my shoulder. "Let yourself lean on us," he said firmly. "On me, on Amma, on Ravi, on your husband. You don't have to do this alone."

His words stayed with me for the rest of the day. I've always been so determined to shoulder burdens on my own, but maybe he's right. Maybe it's time I let myself lean a little.

As we neared home, Nana shared a story from his youth, a small memory of his own struggles and the people who helped him through. It wasn't a grand tale, but it was enough to remind me that strength doesn't always mean standing tall. Sometimes, it means knowing when to accept the hand extended to you.

When we reached the gate, Nana squeezed my hand and gave me one of his rare, warm smiles. "You're doing well, Danya," he said. "I'm proud of you."

Hearing that from him felt like the balm I didn't know I needed. Maybe, just maybe, I'll find my way through this storm after all.

Chapter 10 – Journey to Agra

The Journey to Agra was a mix of excitement and nostalgia for Danya. For years, she had longed to see the Taj Mahal again, but this time, the visit held a special meaning. It wasn't just a family outing; it was a chance to reconnect with her roots and share the experience with her loved ones. Alongside her parents, siblings, husband, children, and the recently arrived Mira and Naureen, the trip felt like a tapestry of past and present woven together.

The group piled into a spacious van early in the morning, chattering away as the streets of Delhi slowly transitioned into the open roads leading toward Agra. Ravi, ever the responsible elder brother, sat in the front with Nana, discussing directions and reminiscing about a visit to the Taj Mahal from their childhood.

"I remember Amma kept scolding me for running too close to the fountain," Arjun chuckled.

"You were a menace back then," Amma quipped from the back seat, her tone laced with affection. "It's a wonder you didn't fall in."

As they drove, Danya felt the gentle hum of her family's laughter envelop her. It was a reprieve from the tension that had gripped her life in recent months. Even Mira and Naureen, who had only recently been drawn into the family's circle, seemed at ease among the warmth and camaraderie.

When the Taj Mahal finally came into view, there was a collective gasp. Its white marble façade shimmered against the pale blue sky, a vision of timeless beauty that seemed almost unreal. The children pressed their faces against the windows, their excitement bubbling over into a chorus of "Look, look!"

Stepping through the gates and onto the sprawling grounds, the family paused for a moment, taking it all in. The vast gardens, the symmetry of the layout, and the majestic mausoleum itself—it was as breathtaking as Danya remembered.

"Let's start with some pictures," Ravi suggested, pulling out his phone.

The group assembled in various formations, taking turns posing in front of the iconic structure. Nana and Amma stood together, their smiles radiant against the backdrop of the Taj Mahal. Danya couldn't help but feel a swell of gratitude as she watched her parents, their love and resilience mirrored in the monument they now stood before.

The children darted around the gardens, marvelling at the fountains and meticulously trimmed hedges. Nihal kept a watchful eye on them, occasionally exchanging amused glances with Ravi and Arjun. Meera, ever the caretaker, fussed over their mother, ensuring Amma stayed hydrated and didn't overexert herself.

Danya found herself walking alongside Mira and Naureen as they explored the inner chambers of the Taj Mahal. The cool marble Beneath their feet and the intricate carvings along the walls transported them to another era. They spoke in hushed tones, marvelling at the artistry and the love story behind the monument.

"It's overwhelming, isn't it?" Mira said, her voice tinged with awe.

"It is," Danya agreed. "And yet, it's calming in a way. A reminder of how love can endure, even though loss."

Their quiet reflection was interrupted when Naureen gestured toward the far end of the chamber. "Is that... Prekshya?"

Danya followed her gaze and felt a spark of recognition. Standing near one of the ornate marbles jalis was Prekshya, an old friend from primary school and a detective by profession. Danya hadn't seen her in years, but the poised, observant figure was unmistakable.

"Prekshya!" Danya called out, her voice carrying through the chamber.

Prekshya turned, her face breaking into a warm smile as she recognized Danya. She made her way over, her sharp eyes scanning the group with curiosity.

"Danya! It's been ages," Prekshya said, embracing her. "What a surprise to see you here!"

The two women exchanged pleasantries before Danya introduced Prekshya to the rest of the group. Mira and Naureen seemed particularly intrigued by the detective, their expressions lighting up with recognition when Danya explained Prekshya's line of work.

After a while, the family regrouped in the gardens, settling on a shaded patch of grass for a short break. The children munched on snacks while the adults chatted, their voices blending into a harmonious hum. Danya found a moment to pull Prekshya aside, her mind racing with possibilities.

"It's good to see you," Danya began, her tone more serious now. "I actually think fate might have brought us together today."

Prekshya raised an eyebrow. "Oh? That sounds intriguing."

Danya quickly filled her in on the situation—Zayd's death, the suspicions surrounding it, and the investigation she and her friends had initiated. She explained the role each of them played, their recent efforts in Delhi, and the lingering questions that refused to leave her mind.

"I know this is a lot to ask," Danya said, her voice hesitant, "but we could use someone with your expertise. We've been doing what we can, but a professional's insight would be invaluable."

Prekshya listened intently, her sharp mind already at work. "This is serious," she said finally. "If you're right about the circumstances of his death, it's more than just a family tragedy. It's criminal. I'll help, Danya. I'll look into this."

Relief washed over Danya, and she thanked Prekshya profusely. The detective promised to connect with the group soon and left them with a sense of renewed purpose.

As the day wore on, the family continued to explore the Taj Mahal, soaking in its beauty and history. Danya found herself walking hand-in-hand with her youngest sibling, Meera, who seemed more subdued than usual.

"Didi," Meera said softly, "do you really think we'll find answers?"

Danya squeezed her sister's hand. "I don't know, Meera. But we have to try. Zayd wouldn't want us to stop searching for the truth."

By the time they left Agra and began their Journey back to Delhi, the family was tired but content. The day had been a whirlwind of emotions, but it had also brought them closer together. For Danya, it was a reminder that even in the midst of uncertainty, there was strength in unity, in love, and in the shared pursuit of justice.

Danya's Diary

Three days. Only three days left before this whirlwind trip to India ends. I can hardly believe how quickly time has flown, how packed these days have been with laughter, love, and moments that will stay with me forever. And yet, there's a bittersweet ache building in my chest. I'm not ready to leave, not ready to say goodbye to everything this trip has meant.

Today, I woke up before the sun rose. The house was quiet, save for the faint hum of the ceiling fan and the occasional creak of the floorboards. As I sat by the window, sipping a steaming cup of chai Amma had made the night before and left for me in a thermos, I watched the city slowly come to life. Delhi is chaotic, vibrant, and relentless, but in the early morning hours, it holds a kind of peace. The world feels softer then, like it's letting you catch your breath before the day starts.

These past few weeks have been a kaleidoscope of emotions. Being here, in the place that shaped me, surrounded by the people I love most, has been healing in ways I didn't expect. It's also been overwhelming. There's been so much to process, so many memories stirred up, and so many responsibilities weighing on my shoulders.

Yesterday's visit to the Taj Mahal was a reminder of how fleeting time can feel. Standing there, staring at that monument of love and loss, I couldn't help but think of Zayd. He's been in my thoughts constantly, a shadow I can't shake. Sometimes it feels like he's still here, watching over us, urging us to find the answers he couldn't.

And then there's my family. Amma and Nana have been nothing short of incredible. Amma, with her quiet strength and endless reserves of love, has this way of making everything seem manageable, even when it's not. And Nana, with his wisdom and calm demeanour, always knows what to say to steady me. I've leaned on them so much during this trip, more than I thought I would.

Ravi has been my rock, as he always is. There's something so comforting about having an elder brother like him—someone who carries the weight of the world on his shoulders so you don't have to. He's been such a pillar of support, quietly ensuring everything runs smoothly without ever drawing attention to himself.

Arjun and Meera, my younger siblings, have brought so much Joy to this trip. Arjun, with his sharp wit and endless curiosity, keeps us all on our toes. Meera, sweet and thoughtful, has this uncanny ability to sense when someone needs a kind word or a moment of quiet. Watching her play with my children has been a gift—she's so gentle with them, so full of love.

Nihal, my husband, has been incredible through all of this. He's patient and understanding, even when I've been distracted or overwhelmed. He knows when to give me space and when to pull me close, and I don't think I could have navigated this trip without him. Watching him bond with Amma and Nana has been one of the highlights of this Journey.

And my children... oh, how they've thrived here. There's something about being surrounded by family that brings out the best in them. They've been soaking up stories from their grandparents, running around with their uncles and aunt, and just being their happy, curious selves. It's a Joy to watch.

But amidst all the Joy and connection, there's the ever-present weight of what we're here to do. Mira and Naureen have been invaluable, their perspectives and expertise adding so much to the investigation. Having them here feels like a bridge between my old life and the one I've built now—a reminder that we don't have to face this alone.

And then there's Prekshya. Running into her at the Taj Mahal felt like fate, like a sign that we're on the right path. She's already started digging into things, asking the kind of pointed questions only she can. There's a fire in her, a determination that's both inspiring and reassuring. I'm so glad I got her number.

The clock is ticking, and I feel the pressure mounting. Three days isn't much time, but it's enough to take the next steps. We've been working on gathering information, coordinating with everyone back home, and planning our approach. There's still so much to do, so many pieces to put together, but I'm determined to make the most of the time we have left.

I keep reminding myself why we're doing this—why we can't give up, no Matter how daunting it feels. Zayd deserves the truth. His family deserves answers. And if there's even a chance, we can uncover what really happened, we owe it to him to try.

As I sit here, writing this, I can hear the faint sounds of my children stirring in the next room. Soon, the house will be alive with activity—Amma bustling in the kitchen, Nana reading the paper, Ravi planning the day's itinerary. We have another busy day ahead, and I know it will be filled with moments I'll treasure long after we've left.

Three days. That's all we have left here, and I intend to make every second count.

Chapter 11: Wisdom in Old Friendships

The morning sun filtered through the trees as Danya and her family piled into a rented van, the air buzzing with excitement and anticipation. They were heading to visit an old family friend, Professor Sundar. A renowned scholar and historian, he had been a close companion of Nana's since their college days. Over the years, he had become like an uncle to Danya and her siblings—a guiding figure whose wisdom was sought in moments of uncertainty.

The drive to Sundar Uncle's modest yet elegant home on the outskirts of Delhi was a Journey steeped in nostalgia. Nana spoke animatedly to Nihal about the days he and Sundar Uncle spent debating history, literature, and politics late into the night.

"Ah, Sundar," Nana mused with a fond smile, "he was always the philosopher among us. While I tackled medicine, he lived in the pages of dusty old books. A man of incredible knowledge."

Amma, sitting beside Nana, chimed in, "And a heart of gold. Sundar helped us so much when Ravi was born. We were just starting out in Delhi, and he ensured we never felt alone."

Danya smiled as she listened. She remembered Sundar Uncle well from her childhood. He always seemed to know the answers to every question, no Matter how big or small. To her young mind, he had been a larger-than-life figure.

When they arrived, the family spilled out of the van, stretching their legs and marvelling at the lush garden surrounding Sundar Uncle's house. The house itself was a charming mix of old-world charm and modern practicality. Books were stacked neatly on the windowsills, and a veranda with wicker chairs welcomed visitors.

Sundar Uncle, now in his seventies, greeted them warmly, his smile as bright as ever. His hair had turned completely silver, but his sharp eyes and robust voice betrayed no sign of his age.

"Ramesh! Asha!" he exclaimed, embracing them both. "And these must be your brood! My, how they've grown!"

Danya introduced Nihal and her children, who were immediately drawn to Sundar Uncle's gentle demeanour. He led them inside, ushering everyone into a spacious sitting room adorned with framed photographs and shelves upon shelves of books.

Over cups of steaming filter coffee and plates of homemade murukku, the family settled into comfortable conversation. Ravi and Arjun spoke with Sundar Uncle about Delhi's changing landscape, while Meera listened intently, occasionally chiming in with her own observations.

Danya, meanwhile, found herself drawn to the scholar's wisdom for a deeper reason. As the chatter flowed around her, she leaned forward and said, "Uncle, there's something I'd like to discuss with you. Something important."

Sundar Uncle's expression softened, and he nodded knowingly. "Of course, my dear. Let's talk."

He led Danya, Nihal, Mira, and Naureen to a smaller study at the back of the house. The room was lined with bookshelves, and a large wooden desk sat in the centre, cluttered with papers, a globe, and a magnifying glass. It smelled faintly of parchment and ink, a comforting scent.

Once they were seated, Danya began hesitantly. "Uncle, I've been grappling with something. You know about Zayd, my mentor. His death has raised questions that won't leave me alone. There's a suspicion... something that doesn't feel right about the circumstances."

Sundar Uncle's brow furrowed, and he adjusted his glasses. "Go on, child."

"We've been working to uncover the truth. There are too many inconsistencies in his medical history, his death—too many unanswered questions. But it's more than that. There are... people we suspect might have played a role in his demise. We need to know if we're on the right path."

Mira and Naureen added details about their ongoing examinations and the connections they were piecing together. Sundar Uncle listened intently, occasionally nodding or asking pointed questions.

"Danya," he said finally, his tone deliberate, "the pursuit of truth is never without risk. But it's also never without reward. Zayd Hasan was a man of integrity, and if you believe his death was not as it seemed, then you owe it to him and his family to find the answers."

Danya felt a lump rise in her throat. "Uncle, you always seem to know the right thing to say. But how do we proceed? How do we ensure we're doing the right thing without jeopardizing everything?"

Sundar Uncle leaned back in his chair, stroking his chin thoughtfully. "You proceed with caution but also with determination. Ramesh has often told me how resilient you are, Danya. Use that strength. Surround yourself with people who can guide you, like these wonderful friends you've brought along. And never underestimate the power of knowledge. The answers are often hiding in plain sight; you just need to look in the right places."

Mira spoke up, "That's what we're hoping to do. The pieces are scattered, but we're starting to see a pattern."

"Then focus on those patterns," Sundar Uncle advised. "And Danya, remember this: even if you don't find what you're looking for, the Journey itself can reveal truths you never expected. Trust in that."

The conversation stretched on, delving into history, philosophy, and even mythology as Sundar Uncle drew parallels between their quest and age-old tales of justice and perseverance. His words were a balm to Danya's restless mind, offering clarity and purpose.

As they rejoined the rest of the family in the sitting room, the atmosphere was lighter, more relaxed. Sundar Uncle took a moment to share stories from his youth, drawing laughter from everyone.

When it was time to leave, Danya felt a deep sense of gratitude. As she hugged Sundar Uncle goodbye, she said, "Thank you for everything, Uncle. You've given me more than advice today; you've given me hope."

He patted her hand gently. "Hope, my dear, is the foundation of all great endeavours. Go with it, and you'll find your way."

As the van pulled away from Sundar Uncle's house, Danya looked back, her heart full. This visit had been more than a reunion; it had been a turning point, a reminder that even in the face of uncertainty, wisdom and love could light the path forward.

Danya's Diary

Two days. Just two days left in this whirlwind of a trip, and I find myself grasping at every fleeting moment, trying to hold on to the pieces of a Journey that has been both healing and challenging.

Today was quieter compared to the chaos of the past week, but in some ways, it felt heavier. The reality of leaving Delhi—and all that has come with this trip—is beginning to settle in. This city, with its relentless energy and layered history, has always been more than just a place to me. It's home, no Matter how many years I've spent away.

Amma and Nana have been different these past few days, a quiet shift in their demeanour that I can't quite place. Maybe it's the weight of my revelations, or maybe it's just the inevitability of time passing too quickly. Nana took me for a walk yesterday, and his words still linger in my mind. He told me to find the balance between truth and compassion, to never lose sight of the people behind the facts. It's advice I needed to hear.

Today, Ravi and Nihal were deep in conversation for much of the afternoon. Seeing them bond warms my heart. Ravi has always been more than just a brother—he's been a rock, a source of strength I've leaned on more times than I can count. And Nihal? He's stepped into my family's world so seamlessly. Watching him Joke with Arjun and indulge Meera's endless questions reminds me why I fell in love with him in the first place.

I spent a lot of time with Amma today. We cooked together in the kitchen, just like old times. She made her famous mango pickle, and I tried my best to replicate her dosas. She laughed at my attempts, and for a moment, it felt like nothing had changed—like I was still the girl who would hover by her side, stealing spoonfuls of chutney when she wasn't looking.

But things have changed, haven't they? Life has a way of layering itself, one experience over the next, until the simplicity of childhood feels like a distant dream. And yet, there are constants—like Amma's laughter, the way Nana's eyes light up when he's telling a story, the camaraderie of siblings who know you better than anyone else ever could.

We all sat together in the living room after dinner, Mira and Naureen included. The kids were sprawled on the floor, their laughter filling the room as they played some board game they'd brought along. For a moment, I allowed myself to forget about the investigation, about the questions that still hover unanswered.

But only for a moment.

Tomorrow, we meet Prekshya again. She's been digging into some details for us, and there's a part of me that's bracing for what she might uncover. The weight of this search for truth grows heavier by the day, and while I'm grateful for the allies we've found along the way—Mira, Naureen, even Sundar Uncle—it's exhausting.

I can feel the toll it's taking on everyone, especially Nihal. He's been so patient, so supportive, but I see the concern in his eyes when he thinks I'm not looking. He knows how much this means to me, and I love him even more for standing by me, for letting me chase this even when it feels like chasing shadows.

The kids, thankfully, have been blissfully unaware of most of it. I've tried my best to shield them, to keep this trip as normal as possible for them. It hasn't been easy, but their Joy has been a constant reminder of what really Matters.

And now, as I sit here writing, the house is quiet. Everyone else has gone to bed, but I needed this time to reflect, to process.

In two days, we'll board that flight back home, leaving Delhi behind. But I know I won't really leave it behind—not the city, not this family, not the questions that have consumed me since Zayd's death. They'll come with me, woven into the fabric of who I am and who I'm becoming.

For now, though, I'll hold onto these last moments here. I'll savour Amma's cooking, Nana's stories, the chaos of siblings who still know how to bicker like kids, and the love of a family that has anchored me through every storm.

Two days. It feels too short, but maybe it's just enough.

Chapter 12: The Last Day

The morning sun filtered through the thin curtains of Amma and Nana's home, casting a warm glow that seemed at odds with the bittersweet air that hung over the house. Danya sat on the edge of her bed, staring at her half-packed suitcase. The last day of their trip had arrived, and she wasn't ready.

Voices echoed from the kitchen downstairs—Amma giving instructions, Ravi teasing her about something, and the clatter of pots as breakfast preparations got underway. The scent of freshly made chai and dosas wafted upstairs, pulling Danya from her thoughts. She made her way down, savouring the familiar chaos of home.

"Didi!" Meera called out, spotting her from the staircase. "Finally! Amma's been asking for you."

Danya smiled at her younger sister, who was bustling around the dining area, helping set the table. It was moments like these, surrounded by family, that made leaving so hard.

Amma was in her usual spot by the stove, flipping dosas with practiced ease. She looked up as Danya entered the kitchen. "Ah, there you are! You're not escaping without eating a full breakfast today," she declared, her tone both loving and firm.

"Yes, Amma," Danya replied with a grin, leaning in to kiss her on the cheek.

Nihal and Ravi were already seated at the table, deep in conversation about something Danya couldn't quite catch. Her children were perched on a nearby sofa, engrossed in a cartoon playing on the TV. Nana sat in his favourite chair, sipping his chai and reading the morning newspaper, a picture of contentment.

The meal was lively, filled with chatter and laughter. Ravi recounted a story from his university days, drawing laughs from everyone at the table. Meera chimed in with her own anecdotes, while Arjun, ever the quiet one, smiled faintly at their antics. It felt like every moment was magnified, every interaction holding the weight of impending goodbyes.

After breakfast, the family decided to spend the day together, soaking in every last bit of time they had. Danya suggested a visit to Lodhi Garden, a favourite spot from her childhood, and the idea was met with enthusiastic agreement.

The sprawling gardens were as beautiful as Danya remembered, the historic tombs standing tall amidst lush greenery. The children ran ahead, their laughter ringing out as they played hide-and-seek among the trees. Danya walked hand-in-hand with Nihal, her heart full as she watched her family.

Amma and Nana strolled leisurely, Nana pausing every so often to point out a bird or flower that caught his eye. Ravi and Arjun followed behind, deep in discussion about some political topic, while Meera trailed close to Amma, peppering her with questions about old family stories.

As the afternoon stretched on, they found a quiet spot to sit and share a picnic. Amma had packed everyone's favourite snacks, and the simple meal turned into yet another lively family gathering. Stories flowed freely, the conversation shifting effortlessly between memories of the past and hopes for the future.

But Beneath the laughter, Danya felt the weight of the moment. She knew she'd soon be back on a plane, leaving this world behind once again. It wasn't just the physical distance that pained her—it was the sense of leaving a part of herself behind each time she said goodbye.

As the sun dipped lower in the sky, painting the garden in hues of gold and orange, the family returned home. There was a quietness now, a shared understanding that the day was nearing its end.

Back at the house, Amma pulled Danya aside. "Beta," she said softly, her hands resting gently on Danya's shoulders. "I know you have so much on your mind right now. But remember, you are never alone in this. We are here for you, always."

Tears pricked Danya's eyes as she nodded. "Thank you, Amma. I don't know what I'd do without you and Nana."

Later that evening, as the house quieted down, the family gathered in the living room for one final moment together. Amma brought out a photo album, one that Danya hadn't seen in years. They flipped through the pages, revisiting memories of childhood birthdays, family vacations, and simple moments captured in grainy photographs.

Nihal looked over Danya's shoulder, smiling as he pointed out a particularly embarrassing picture of her from her teenage years. "You never told me about this phase," he teased, earning a playful shove from Danya.

Even the children were captivated by the album, listening intently as Nana narrated the stories behind each picture. It was a perfect end to the day, a reminder of the love and history that bound them all together.

As the clock ticked closer to midnight, Danya began her final round of goodbyes. Each hug felt heavier than the last, each word of farewell laced with unspoken emotion.

Amma held her tightly, whispering, "Take care of yourself, beta. And don't forget to call us when you land."

Nana, ever stoic, gave her a firm handshake before pulling her into a hug. "We'll see you soon," he said simply, though his voice was thick with emotion.

Ravi, Arjun, and Meera were no less emotional, each promising to visit soon. Nihal and the children said their own goodbyes, the kids reluctant to leave their beloved grandparents and extended family.

Finally, as they stepped into the car that would take them to the airport, Danya looked back at the house one last time. Amma and Nana stood at the doorway, waving, their faces illuminated by the porch light.

Danya waved back, her heart full and heavy all at once. This was always the hardest part—leaving. But she reminded herself that this wasn't the end. The bonds of family, the love that held them together, would remain no Matter the distance.

As the car pulled away, Danya turned to Nihal, who squeezed her hand reassuringly. "We'll be back," he said softly.

And Danya knew he was right. This wasn't goodbye. Not really.

Danya's Diary

The last day in India. It feels surreal even as I write those words. How has time moved so quickly? It seems just yesterday we were stepping off the plane, greeted by Amma's warm hug and Nana's steady presence. And now, in a Matter of hours, we'll be back on another plane, leaving behind this world that feels so much like home.

Today was an emotional whirlwind. We started the day with Amma insisting that I eat a full breakfast before anything else. She wouldn't let me skip even a bite of the dosa, her gentle scolding making me laugh despite the lump in my throat. It's these small moments—her fussing, Nana quietly handing me a second cup of chai—that make everything feel like it's going to be okay. But today, there was a strange undercurrent of sadness Beneath it all.

I had promised myself that I would make the most of these last few days with my family, but now, knowing the end was near, it felt like I was running out of time. The thought of leaving made my chest tighten, a sense of loss creeping in. We all felt it, even if no one said the words aloud. The quiet understanding that this trip, this time, was special in ways that we may never be able to recreate.

Nihal could tell I was struggling with the thought of leaving. He's always so attuned to me, able to sense my moods without me saying anything. As we packed the last of our things, he squeezed my hand, offering a comforting smile. "We'll come back," he said softly, and I nodded, not trusting my voice. It's not the same, though. Coming back won't be the same. The feeling of being home, surrounded by family, has a weight to it that no visit can replace.

The children were busy running around, playing with their cousins and teasing each other, but I noticed they, too, had a quiet energy about them. Perhaps they sensed the significance of the moment as well. They're so resilient, always so full of life, but today there was a tenderness in their interactions with everyone, like they were trying to hold onto this place too.

Nana took me aside for a walk before lunch. He's always had a way of pulling me into conversation when I need it most. As we strolled through the garden, I could feel the weight of the last few days in his silence. Finally, he spoke.

"Danya, I know how much this trip has meant to you," he said, his voice steady, but with an underlying softness that only he has. "Your Amma and I have watched you grow up, become a woman, a wife, a mother, and now... someone who carries so much of the world on her shoulders. But no Matter where you go, know that you will always have a place here."

I blinked back tears. I've heard him say something like this before, but today, it felt different. Real. Final. My heart aches, the thought of leaving them behind gnawing at me.

"I will always carry this with me, Nana," I told him, my voice barely above a whisper. "This place, this family, it's part of me. And no Matter where I go, I will never forget the feeling of being home."

He smiled, but it was tinged with sadness too. "It's not about forgetting, Danya. It's about remembering. And knowing that home isn't just a place—it's the people you love."

As we returned to the house, the mood shifted. The time had come for goodbyes, or at least for the acknowledgment that the time together was drawing to a close. I hugged Amma one last time, letting her hold me a little longer than usual. Her hands were warm, her embrace enveloping, and I allowed myself to sink into it, letting go of the uncertainty, the guilt, the fear of leaving.

"I'm so proud of you," she said, her voice thick with emotion. "And I know your father is too. We're always with you, Danya."

I wanted to say more, to express everything that was in my heart, but the words stuck in my throat. I just nodded, hoping she understood.

Later, we had a quiet dinner with the whole family. It was a simple meal, but it felt like a feast. Laughter filled the air, and for a few hours, we were able to pretend that things were still as they should be—that this wasn't the last night, that this wasn't goodbye. But the weight of it all hung there, unspoken, in the air around us.

I caught myself looking at each face at the table—Nihal, the kids, my parents, my siblings—and I committed their features to memory. This trip had been a reminder of the importance of family, of connection, and how fragile time can be.

As I sit here now, writing this, I can feel the heaviness in my chest. I don't know how I'll leave, how I'll get on that plane tomorrow and walk away from this place that has shaped me so completely. But I know one thing: I will carry this love, this home, with me. No Matter where life takes us next.

Tomorrow, we leave. But for today, I'll hold onto every moment.

I just wish we had more time.

Chapter 13: The First Flight Back

The last leg of their trip had begun, and Danya couldn't help but feel a sense of finality as they boarded the plane, the hum of the engines a stark reminder that their time in India was over. As she settled into her seat, her fingers lightly tracing the armrest, the reality of the situation began to sink in. They were headed back, and though there was comfort in knowing they'd return home soon, there was also an ache—a feeling that they were leaving something precious behind.

Nihal sat next to her, a quiet presence as always. The children had already settled into their seats by the window, their excitement over the flight still palpable despite the exhaustion that tugged at their eyelids. Mira and Naureen, sitting ahead of them in the row just across the aisle, were also preparing for the next leg of the Journey, each lost in their own thoughts.

It wasn't long before the flight attendants made their way through the aisles, greeting the passengers with warm smiles and a professional efficiency that could only come from experience. Danya wasn't paying much attention at first—her mind was still lingering on the conversations, the goodbyes, and the deep conversations she had with her parents and siblings over the past few days. But something caught her eye as two of the flight attendants walked past.

The first, a woman with short dark hair and a soft but confident smile, locked eyes with Danya for a moment before recognizing her. "Danya?" she asked, her voice carrying just the right touch of familiarity.

Danya blinked in surprise. It was hard to believe it at first. "Mai?" she asked, her voice betraying her disbelief.

Mai grinned, her smile widening. "It's been a while, hasn't it?" She glanced over her shoulder at the other flight attendant, who had paused as well, clearly curious about the interaction.

The second flight attendant, a taller woman with light blonde hair tied back in a neat ponytail, gave Danya a warm smile. "Elsie," she said, offering a friendly wave. "How are you? I didn't realize you were on this flight!"

Danya's heart skipped a beat as she realized just who these women were. Mai and Elsie were two of her childhood friends, the same girls who had been in the same swimming lessons with her all those years ago. They hadn't seen each other since their teenage years, when life had pulled them in different directions. Back then, the three of them had been inseparable during their summer swimming lessons—racing each other through the lanes, learning how to dive, and sharing endless jokes by the poolside.

She hadn't thought of those days in so long. How strange to meet them again, not at a local pool or during some spontaneous gathering, but in the middle of a flight halfway across the world.

"Mai, Elsie," Danya said, her voice thick with emotion. "I can't believe it! What are the odds?"

"We could say the same about you," Elsie replied, still smiling. "The last time we saw each other, we were kids. I didn't even know you were on this flight. Small world, isn't it?"

Danya laughed, feeling a sudden rush of nostalgia. "You've both changed, of course. But not in a way that I didn't recognize you immediately."

The conversation quickly turned to the years between then and now. Mai and Elsie had both become flight attendants, traveling the world with their jobs. Their paths had crossed many times, each one recounting a new experience or an adventure they'd been on. It was funny to hear them talk about their careers, the worlds they'd seen, and the people they'd met, all the while recalling the days of childhood swimming lessons, when the world had seemed much smaller.

"We all used to swim together at that swimming centre back in Wolverhampton," Mai said, her eyes sparkling as she recalled the memories. "Do you remember that one summer when we all tried to beat each other to the deep end? We must've been about, what? Ten? Eleven?"

Danya laughed, the memories flooding back. "I think I was the last one to ever get the hang of sculling, but I remember how competitive we all were. It was the highlight of the summer every year."

"Yeah, and the pranks we used to pull!" Elsie added, shaking her head. "That was half the fun. We never really got in trouble for it, but I don't think the instructor ever knew who left the rubber duck in his swimming cap." She winked at Danya, as if sharing a secret that had remained between them all these years.

The trio talked easily, as if no time had passed. They reminisced about their families, shared stories about their travels, and laughed about their adventures. For Danya, the conversation was a welcome distraction from the emotional weight of the Journey. It felt good to laugh again, to remember a simpler time, even if only for a few moments.

As the flight progressed, the crew attended to the passengers with their usual efficiency, but there was a warmth now, a familiarity between them that wasn't there before. Danya felt a sense of comfort, as if this unexpected reunion was a reminder of the life she had left behind, a life that was still very much a part of her, even as she navigated new chapters of her story.

Nihal leaned over at one point, his voice soft as he whispered, "It's nice to see you so happy, love. I can tell this means a lot to you."

Danya smiled at him, appreciating his understanding. "It does," she said quietly. "It's strange, isn't it? To meet someone from the past, someone who knows you when you were younger. It's like a piece of you is back for a moment."

Mai and Elsie stopped by a few more times during the flight, checking in on Danya and catching up as much as they could in between their duties. They shared more memories, more laughter, and even some advice about the upcoming stop in the Middle East. They promised to stay in touch, though Danya couldn't help but feel that the reunion, as lovely as it was, was bittersweet.

As the plane descended toward the Middle East for a brief layover, Danya gazed out of the window, her thoughts returning to the future and all that lay ahead. But for the moment, she felt connected to the past in a way that she hadn't in years.

"Take care, Danya. We'll call you once you arrive in the UK," Mai called out as she moved toward the front of the plane, her voice warm and filled with genuine affection.

"I will. You too," Danya replied with a smile, knowing that this unexpected meeting would be one of the lasting memories of her trip.

Danya's Diary

It feels so surreal now, sitting here in this quiet airport lounge during our layover. The trip is almost over, and there's just this heavy sense of inevitability weighing on me. In just a few hours, we'll be boarding the flight back home, and I can already feel the mix of emotions rushing in.

I think about everything that's happened during this trip, everything we've learned and experienced. It's been a whirlwind, filled with so many moments that I didn't anticipate. I didn't expect to run into Mai and Elsie. Of course, it's been years since we saw each other, but I never imagined we'd reconnect like this, in the middle of a flight, halfway across the world. The memories we shared as kids, swimming together during those summer lessons, seem so distant now, but they're still there—like pieces of me that never really faded.

I've spent so much time reflecting on how much has changed since then. I'm no longer that carefree girl in the pool, laughing with my friends, looking forward to the next race. Life is different now, and yet, moments like today remind me of the past, of the simpler days before everything got complicated.

But even with the unexpected reunion, there's this deep sense of relief. We're almost home. After all the emotional upheaval, the heartache, and the intense questions about what happened to Zayd, it will be nice to get back to our lives. Of course, there's still so much to figure out, but being back in familiar surroundings will at least give me some sense of control.

I've been thinking a lot about Zayd, too. He's been such a rock throughout all of this, always there to support me, even when things seemed impossible. It's hard for me to express how much that means—how much he means to me. I feel like we've been through so much together, and yet, it's not always easy to put everything into words. But in these quiet moments, when we're traveling together, when it's just us, I can feel the weight of everything we've endured. It's a strange, silent bond that ties us together more than I realize.

The kids are doing okay too. They've been incredibly resilient during the trip, handling everything better than I expected. I think they've come to understand that life can be unpredictable, but they're adjusting. Sometimes I see little flashes of worry in their eyes, but for the most part, they've kept their spirits up, and that's been a comfort.

Mira and Naureen have been wonderful, too. I know they came on this trip to support me, but in many ways, it's felt like they've supported each other as well. There's something special about the way we've all come together during this time. I didn't expect it, but I'm grateful for it. It's strange how hardship can bring people closer, in ways you never anticipated.

As for the investigation, I'm still processing everything. There's so much I don't know, so much I can't even wrap my head around yet. But the fact that Zayd's death was not just a simple tragedy—it's clear that there are more questions than answers right now. I don't know what the future holds, but I know we're not done yet. There's more to uncover, more to understand, and I can't let it go. For his sake, for my sake, and for the sake of everyone who's been affected by this.

I've been talking to people back home, especially about the next steps. The examination of Zayd's body—it's something we'll need to figure out. The people I've been in touch with, including Ajay, have been supportive, but I know this is going to be a long road. Every step feels like it's taking us deeper into unknown territory. I just hope that we can find the truth, no Matter how hard it might be to face.

The flight has been quiet, and it's giving me time to reflect. I think back to the conversations we've had with Mai and Elsie, and it's a reminder that, despite everything, there are still moments of connection that can take us back to simpler times. Maybe those moments can be the small reminders of who we are, even when everything around us seems uncertain.

As the minutes tick by, I can feel myself preparing for the Journey ahead. We'll be landing soon, and I can't help but feel a rush of emotions. There's the relief of returning home, but also the uncertainty of what's next. Whatever happens, I know I'll face it with the support of my family, my friends, and the people who Matter most.

For now, though, I'll just sit here, watching the world outside the window, reflecting on everything that's led me here. The trip is almost over, but the story isn't finished yet.

Chapter 14: The Next Flight

The next leg of their Journey was taking them home, and Danya settled into her seat beside Nihal, her children nestled in the window seats beside them. Mira and Naureen sat just ahead, in the row in front of them. As the plane ascended and the hum of the engines filled the cabin, Danya allowed herself a brief moment to relax. The weight of the past weeks—of the investigations, the emotional rollercoaster, the reunion with her family—was still heavy on her, but for the moment, it was just her family, in their seats, headed toward home.

It was a quiet, peaceful flight at first. Danya glanced at her children, who were already engrossed in their own activities, and then turned her attention to the window, watching the endless expanse of sky stretching out below. Nihal sat quietly beside her, his hand resting gently on hers. They didn't speak much, but Danya could feel his presence beside her—constant, supportive, unwavering. After everything, she was glad to have him by her side.

A few hours into the flight, there was a sudden shift in the air. The sound of footsteps down the aisle grew more frequent, and Danya looked up to see a flight attendant walking briskly toward the front of the cabin. Her gaze followed the attendant's movement, and that was when she noticed someone else in the galley area—a familiar face.

It was Immy, her childhood friend from their choir days. Immy was always the one with the infectious laugh, the one who could always get the choir to sing just a little louder, with more heart. They hadn't spoken in years, but the moment Danya's eyes locked with hers, a flood of memories came rushing back.

Immy looked up and caught her gaze, smiling with recognition. A moment later, she was walking toward Danya's seat.

"Well, well, if it isn't Danya!" Immy said, her voice warm and full of that same energy Danya remembered so well. "What are the odds? I can't believe we're on the same flight!"

Danya smiled, feeling the comforting pull of familiarity. "Immy! I didn't expect to see you here. I'm on my way back from India with my family."

Immy nodded, a bit of surprise in her eyes. "I'm in the galley today. I'm actually crew for this flight. But it's so good to see you! How's everything?"

Before Danya could answer, the intercom crackled to life, and the voice of a flight attendant filled the cabin.

"Passengers, due to a medical emergency, is there a doctor on board? Please assist if you can."

Danya felt a jolt of adrenaline shoot through her. The voice was unmistakable—Evie, another childhood friend from their choir days. Though they hadn't stayed connected, Danya could hear Evie's tone, calm but urgent, carrying over the intercom. There was no hesitation in her voice, just clear, steady professionalism. But it was enough to stir something deep inside Danya.

She stood up immediately, looking at Immy. "Is everything okay?"

Immy's expression shifted, a flicker of concern passing across her face. "I don't know. I just heard it too. Let me check."

Immy turned and hurried toward the galley, disappearing behind the curtain that separated the business class section from the rest of the cabin. Danya's pulse quickened. She knew that whatever the emergency was, it had to be serious if Evie was making the announcement. She had never heard her friend sound quite so urgent before.

Danya moved toward the rear of the plane, weaving through the aisles, her eyes scanning the cabin. That's when she saw it—a commotion in the back row of economy class, a group of passengers gathered around someone in distress.

A flight attendant was at the scene, trying to calm a young girl who was slumped in her seat, her face pale, her breathing erratic. Danya's heart sank as she stepped closer. The girl looked no older than sixteen or seventeen, her eyes wide with panic, her chest rising and falling rapidly.

"Please, can you help?" one of the passengers asked, almost pleading. "She's not responding properly."

Danya knelt beside the girl and placed a hand gently on her shoulder. "What happened?"

One of the flight attendants, a woman with a nervous expression, stepped aside to let Danya take control. "We don't know. She was fine a few moments ago, and then she just started hyperventilating. Her heart rate's elevated, but she's barely able to speak."

Danya nodded, assessing the situation. "What's her name?"

"Julianna," the flight attendant said quickly. "She's been traveling alone. We're trying to reach her family."

Danya could see the terror in Julianna's eyes as she struggled to breathe, the shallow, fast breaths making her chest heave. It looked like an acute panic attack, but Danya wasn't willing to rule out other possibilities. She needed to assess her carefully. "Julianna, it's okay. I'm a doctor. I'm here to help."

Julianna blinked, the fear still evident in her wide eyes. Danya continued speaking in a soothing tone, trying to calm her. "I need you to take slow, deep breaths with me. In and out, slowly, okay?"

As Julianna tried to follow her instructions, Danya reached for her pulse, feeling the rapid thumping under her fingers. "I'm going to need a couple of things. We need some oxygen and a cold compress. And a space to lay her down."

The attendants moved quickly to comply, helping Danya ease Julianna onto the seat beside her. The air around them was thick with tension, but Danya focused, blocking out the rising panic in her own chest. The oxytocin in her system from helping someone in distress should have calmed her, but instead, she felt a wave of anxiety creep up her spine. Her hands trembled as she gently held Julianna's head, adjusting the oxygen mask over her nose and mouth.

The young girl's breathing began to slow, and the frantic look in her eyes softened just a little. Danya stayed by her side, speaking softly, keeping her calm, as they moved her to an empty row in the front of economy for more space.

As the flight attendants worked to secure the area, Danya continued monitoring Julianna's vitals, making sure the oxygen was helping. The entire situation felt oddly familiar, almost as if she had been in this exact scenario before. Yet, despite her steady presence and the help she was giving, Danya couldn't shake the wave of panic that kept rising within her. The adrenaline from the earlier rush began to fade, leaving behind a hollow feeling in her chest.

Evie appeared moments later, her professional demeanour still intact despite the chaos. "Is she stable?" she asked.

Danya nodded. "She's responding better. We need to keep an eye on her until we land."

Evie gave a quick nod, her face softening with relief. She turned to the intercom to make a new announcement.

"Ladies and gentlemen, we've been able to stabilize the passenger in question. Thank you for your patience. We'll continue to monitor the situation until we land. Once again, we apologize for the interruption, and we appreciate your cooperation."

Danya stayed with Julianna until the plane began its descent, her heart still heavy with the weight of what had just happened. As they touched down in the Middle East, she felt the familiar pang of exhaustion settle over her. She had helped, but the experience had drained her more than she cared to admit.

She met Evie's eyes one more time as they made their way to the front of the plane, and Evie gave her a tired, knowing smile.

"I owe you one, Danya," she said quietly. "You're a lifesaver."

Danya didn't respond right away. She just nodded, feeling the quiet hum of emotion in her chest. Despite the relief she felt in helping someone in need, there was still a sense of unease lingering, as if everything was just beginning to unravel.

Danya's Diary

I can't believe I'm on the way home. It feels like everything from this trip to India has been such a whirlwind. The highs, the lows, all the intense moments that I know I will carry with me for a long time. But right now, as I sit here on this plane, I'm just trying to take it all in and let it settle. Three days left in the trip, and I can't help but reflect on all that's happened.

Nihal is beside me, calm as ever. My children are in the window seats beside us, lost in their own worlds. Mira and Naureen are ahead of us in the row, and I can tell they're excited to get home too. I'm simply happy to be with them, all of us safe, all of us together. It's been a long time since I felt this sense of quiet peace.

The flight started out as normal as can be. There's a comfort in routine, especially when it's a routine you know so well. The sounds of the engines, the dim lights, the soft chatter of other passengers. It was easy to get lost in the simplicity of it, and for a while, that's exactly what I did. I gazed out the window, letting my mind wander.

Then, just a few hours in, something unexpected happened. I saw a familiar face. Immy. I couldn't believe it when I saw her in the galley, walking towards me with that same bright energy I remembered from our childhood choir days. She recognized me almost immediately, and we exchanged a few quick words. It felt like a moment of normalcy amidst the whirlwind of everything else.

But then, just as quickly, the calm was shattered. Evie's voice came over the intercom. I knew immediately something was wrong. Evie was always so composed, so professional. To hear her voice crackling with urgency—it made my stomach drop. And then, the words that sent my heart racing: "Passengers, due to a medical emergency, is there a doctor on board?"

I didn't hesitate. I stood up, and without a second thought, I headed toward the back of the plane, following the voices that were gathering around. There, in the middle of economy class, was a young girl—Julianna. Her face was pale, and her breathing was shallow and quick. Something was wrong, and I could feel it in my bones.

I could tell that the flight attendants were doing their best, but this wasn't something they could handle alone. I knelt beside the girl and immediately started assessing her, asking her to breathe slowly. It wasn't a heart attack, but the panic in her eyes told me she was spiralling into something much worse. A severe panic attack, I thought at first, but I wasn't ruling anything out.

I've dealt with so many medical situations in my life, but this one felt different. Maybe it was the urgency in Evie's voice. Maybe it was the way my hands trembled slightly as I worked to stabilize Julianna. Whatever it was, I couldn't shake the feeling that I wasn't just helping her—I was somehow trying to calm myself too.

With the help of the flight attendants, we managed to move Julianna to an empty row at the front of the cabin. I stayed with her, monitoring her breathing, her pulse. She was still scared, but slowly, she was responding to the oxygen. The quiet weight of it all was overwhelming, but I stayed focused. I had to.

Evie came to check on us soon after, and though she was professional as always, I could see the tension in her face. She made an announcement to the passengers, calming them down, letting them know everything was under control. Her voice sounded so steady over the intercom, but I could tell that she was just as shaken by what had happened as I was.

I didn't stay with Julianna for too long after that. Once she was stable and the flight attendants had everything under control, I returned to my seat. My heart was still pounding, my mind racing. There was a part of me that was proud of what I'd done, but another part of me couldn't ignore the heavy feeling in my chest. I had helped, yes, but something about that experience felt... off.

I'm sitting here now, trying to relax, but I can't shake the feeling that the day's events have left me with more questions than answers. I'm still a bit shaken, even though I know Julianna is okay now. There's something about that rush of adrenaline, the fear of being in an emergency situation, that never really goes away once you've been through it. And despite everything, despite the relief of helping her, I can't ignore the sense of panic that rose in me as I worked.

Maybe I'm just tired. Maybe it's the aftereffects of everything that's happened on this trip. But right now, I'm trying to focus on the good things. The fact that we're all safe, that my family is with me, and that we're almost home. There's just a little more time left before we get there. I want to hold onto the calm moments, the ones when I can just be with my family, and not think about everything that's going on outside of our little bubble.

I miss my family incredibly but I can't wait to get back, to see everyone again, to find some sense of normalcy. But for now, I'll take this quiet moment to reflect. It's the calm before the storm, I suppose. Just a little while longer before we're home.

Chapter 15: The Rest of the Flight

The cabin lights had dimmed, and the soft hum of the engines created a steady rhythm that helped to calm the tension in the air. After the chaos of the medical emergency earlier in the flight, Danya was finally able to settle back into her seat beside Nihal. The children were quietly occupied in their seats, and Mira and Naureen were in the row ahead. It felt like a brief moment of peace, a respite after the whirlwind of events that had unfolded.

Despite the calm, Danya's thoughts were still racing, but there was something comforting about the routine of the flight—the quiet chatter from the passengers, the movement of the crew, the occasional ding of the seatbelt sign as the flight continued its Journey toward its next stop.

A few minutes later, Immy and Evie appeared in business class. They were both still in their uniforms, though they had removed their jackets for a bit of relief after the stressful situation in economy. Immy gave Danya a warm smile as she approached, her face still holding traces of concern from the emergency, but her eyes sparkled with the familiar energy Danya remembered from their younger days.

"Hey, how are you doing?" Immy asked as she sat down beside her, her voice gentle, but with the unmistakable strength of someone who had seen their fair share of turbulence—both literally and figuratively.

Danya smiled back, grateful for her friend's presence. "I'm alright. Just... catching my breath. It's been a long flight, but I'm glad Julianna is okay."

Evie, who had Joined Immy, nodded in agreement. "We all did what we could. It was a close call, but the team worked together. I'm glad you were there to help, Danya. I'm not sure what would've happened without you."

Danya felt a rush of oxytocin—she was always so used to being in control of the situation, but this time, having help from friends who shared her sense of duty was comforting. "I didn't even think about it. I just saw the situation and acted. I'm glad she's alright, though."

Immy looked around, her smile turning into a mischievous grin. "So, you know, we've got a 24-hour layover when we land. It's not much, but we should make the most of it. How about we all spend time together? You, Nihal, and the kids can join us. Maybe grab a bite, see the sights, just take a breather before the next leg of your journey."

Danya's heart lightened at the offer. It was exactly what she needed—time with old friends, time to relax, and most importantly, time to decompress before the next leg of their journey. "That sounds perfect. I could use a little downtime. And the kids will love it too."

Evie grinned, "It'll be fun. We'll show you around, take you to all the places we know, and you can finally get some rest."

The crew members, who were all catching a brief break, chatted for a little longer before they had to return to their duties. Danya and Immy exchanged some more stories from their choir days, and it was a strange, almost surreal feeling to talk to Immy after so many years. It felt like they hadn't skipped a beat, despite everything that had changed in the meantime.

Eventually, as the plane continued its journey, Danya found herself with more time to reflect. The earlier rush of adrenaline from the medical emergency had faded, and she could feel her body responding to the gentle swaying of the plane. She glanced over at Nihal, who had his eyes closed, trying to catch a bit of rest, and she felt a sense of gratitude for this moment of calm.

It wasn't just the chance to hang out with friends that was keeping her spirits up; it was also the knowledge that, in a few hours, they would finally be able to unwind. The thought of exploring a new place with old friends was exciting, and Danya was looking forward to seeing where this unexpected detour would take them.

Mira and Naureen, who had been relatively quiet during the flight, turned around and whispered to Danya. "Are we really going to hang out with them tomorrow? That sounds fun!"

Danya nodded, smiling at their enthusiasm. "Yes, we are. It'll be a nice break, and you will love it too. Just relax and enjoy it. We deserve a little fun after everything that's happened."

As the crew members moved through the cabin, preparing for the next part of the flight, Danya found herself feeling both exhausted and strangely energized. The Journey ahead would bring its own challenges, but for now, she could focus on the present, on the quiet moments shared with friends, on the chance to be with her family, and on the opportunity to finally recharge before the final stretch of the trip.

By the time the flight attendants began their preparations for landing, Danya felt like she had crossed over into a new phase of the trip. She was no longer just focused on the investigation, on the turmoil and the questions that had plagued her for the last few days. For the first time in a while, her mind had cleared, even if just for a little while, and the upcoming layover felt like a much-needed reset.

"Do you think we'll have enough time to actually rest tomorrow?" Nihal asked, his voice soft as he stirred beside her.

"We'll make time," Danya replied with a smile. "We need to. We all need it."

The rest of the flight passed by relatively uneventfully, with the occasional hum of the engines and the soft murmur of voices around them. Danya watched the lights of distant cities flicker far below, her mind at ease for the first time in days. When the plane finally began its descent, Danya felt ready for whatever was coming next, even if she didn't know exactly what it was.

She was with her family. She was with her friends. And for once, she had no answers—just a few hours of peace before the Journey continued. And that, for now, was enough.

Danya's Diary

It's hard to believe that we're only a few hours away from landing. The flight has felt like a mix of chaos and calm, and I've been trying to hold onto every moment of peace. I don't know what it is about this flight, but I've felt oddly at ease. Maybe it's the fact that I'm surrounded by friends I haven't seen in so long, or maybe it's just the relief of helping with that emergency. Even though it was intense, it's comforting to know I can still act under pressure, that I can make a difference when it Matters.

Nihal's been by my side this whole time, just quietly letting me process everything. I'm sure he's exhausted, and so are the kids, but there's a quiet solidarity in this Journey. I feel like we're all just moving forward, one step at a time, even though the future feels so uncertain right now.

When I saw Immy and Evie again, I felt this rush of nostalgia. The last time we were together like this, we were just kids, singing in the choir. So much time has passed, but when I spoke to them, it was like we'd never been apart. They're both incredible women, and I can't help but feel grateful for having them in my life, especially at a time like this.

Immy's idea of us spending time together during our layover is exactly what I need. I'm looking forward to it, even though I know it's just a brief pause before we move on. But for now, I'm letting myself enjoy the thought of relaxing, seeing some sights, and just being present with the people I care about. It's a rare opportunity, and I need to make the most of it.

The children are excited about the layover, of course. They're always eager for an adventure, even if it's just a few hours in a new place. And I'm glad they're so adaptable, so open to whatever comes next. They've been through so much already, and I want to give them this small Joy in the middle of all the uncertainty.

I've been thinking a lot about the past few days—about everything that happened in India, about the investigation. But as the plane cruises on, I've found myself pushing those thoughts aside, just for a little while. There will be time for all of that later. Right now, it's about being with Nihal, the kids, Immy, and Evie. It's about allowing myself to breathe.

I'll admit, though, I feel a bit of guilt. There's still so much I want to uncover, so many questions that are left unanswered. But I know I can't keep chasing them every minute of the day. I have to trust that things will unfold in their own time. For now, I'm here, and I'm focusing on what I can control—my own peace, my family's well-being, and the chance to recharge.

The flight attendants have started preparing for landing, and I can't help but feel a twinge of excitement. We'll have our layover soon, and while it won't last long, it's a chance for all of us to just step away from the noise for a moment. I'm ready for whatever the next few hours will bring, but I'm also content to sit in this moment for a while longer.

Tomorrow, we'll dive back into it all—the investigation, the unanswered questions, everything. But tonight, we rest. Tonight, I have my family, my friends, and a little peace, and that's enough for me right now.

Chapter 16: The Meeting

Danya entered the conference room with a heavy heart, the weight of everything that had transpired over the past few weeks lingering in the back of her mind. The jetlag from the long flights hadn't quite worn off, but it was the emotional toll that had left her drained. As she walked into the room, she was greeted by the familiar faces of the people who had been by her side throughout this investigation—friends, family, and colleagues alike. She took a deep breath and forced a smile, trying to remain composed.

Naureen was already there, sitting at the table, her expression serious but calm. Kanchana, always steady and clear-headed, sat beside her, her eyes scanning a folder of medical documents. Elodie, Laila, and Omar were talking quietly in one corner, and Danya's eyes met each of theirs in turn. Rami and Sara had already settled in, their chairs slightly turned to face the front where Danya would be presenting. Samira sat next to Rami, a slight frown etched on her face as she flipped through her notes.

Mira Quaid, always the diligent observer, was at the far end of the room. She gave Danya a warm nod of acknowledgment. Mia Armstrong, sat with her arms crossed, her expression thoughtful.

Danya moved to the front, setting her briefcase down on the table. She felt the room settle into silence as everyone turned their attention to her. She had always been a planner, a thinker, but today, more than ever, she knew that this meeting was crucial. Zayd's death—her husband's untimely passing—had brought them all together, and now it was time to take the next steps.

"Thank you all for coming," Danya began, her voice steady despite the heaviness in her chest. "I know it's been a lot to handle, and I don't take it lightly that you've all been so invested in figuring out what happened to Zayd."

She paused for a moment, her eyes moving across the room, meeting each of their gazes. "I called this meeting today to discuss the next phase. We've made a lot of progress, but there's still so much left to do, and I need your expertise, your support, and your focus."

Naureen gave her an encouraging nod, while Kanchana leaned forward, her posture alert. Elodie was taking notes, and Laila's eyes were focused on Danya, waiting for her to continue. Danya took another breath, her mind flickering back to the aircraft, to the discussions they'd had in the lounge, and to the sense of urgency that still lingered in her heart.

"We've already talked about some preliminary examinations," Danya said, her voice gaining strength. "But now we need to take it further. I'm sure we're all thinking the same thing. Zayd's death wasn't just a tragic accident. I know some of you might still have doubts, but the more I look at everything—the medical records, the timing, the way things unfolded—the more I feel like something went wrong. Something beyond what we initially believed."

Mia, who had been quiet until now, spoke up, her voice measured. "What exactly are we looking for, Danya? What do you think went wrong?"

Danya turned toward Mia, feeling the weight of her words settle. "I think Zayd was murdered. I don't have solid proof yet, but the evidence points to foul play. We need to look deeper into the circumstances surrounding his death. The illness that took him, the speed of his decline—it just doesn't add up. We have to investigate every angle."

The room was silent for a moment, the gravity of Danya's statement hanging in the air. Everyone exchanged glances, processing what she had said. Then, one by one, they nodded, all in agreement, though the uncertainty was still palpable.

"We've been talking about the types of examinations we need," Naureen said, breaking the silence. "But it's important to remember that we also need to consider all possible angles. Not just the medical side of things."

Danya nodded, turning toward Naureen. "Exactly. We need to keep our minds open. We can't discount anything. But I believe that the first step is conducting further medical exams."

Kanchana looked up from her notes, her brow furrowed in thought. "We talked about doing a deeper investigation into the medical records. That includes looking at Zayd's treatment history, the medications he was given, and any inconsistencies with the diagnoses we were given. It's a lot to go through, but we need to get all the details."

"Yes," Danya replied, "I agree. But we also need the radiologists involved, too. Molly and Paula, I want you to help us with the imaging. We need to see if there's anything in Zayd's scans that we missed or that's been overlooked. Any subtle signs of something more."

Molly, the radiologist, nodded. "We'll go through the records and see what we can find. We'll take a close look at everything—no stone unturned."

"And then," Danya continued, "we'll proceed with further diagnostic tests. We talked about using more invasive methods if necessary. Nasoendoscope, laryngoscopy, and pharyngeal assessments. Naureen, you'll handle the pharynx tests, and Kanchana, you'll work on the nasoendoscope with the team. Elodie, Laila, and Sara—you'll focus on the laryngoscopy."

There were murmurs of agreement around the table as everyone took in the plan. They had all seen what had happened to Zayd, the rapid decline, the strange symptoms, but now they were committed to finding the truth. Danya could see the resolve in their eyes—their dedication to uncovering the secrets that had been hidden.

Rami, who had been quiet until now, spoke up. "It's going to be a lot of work, Danya. A lot of careful coordination. But we're all in. We'll find out what happened."

Samira, sitting beside Rami, nodded. "We'll be with you every step of the way."

Danya felt the weight of the situation ease a little, knowing that she had the support of everyone in that room. They weren't just colleagues or friends; they were all in this together, working for the same goal. To uncover the truth about Zayd's death.

"I know we can do this," Danya said, her voice thick with emotion. "We have to do this for Zayd. For his memory. For all of us."

Everyone in the room gave their agreement, and Danya felt a sense of solidarity settle over her. They would do whatever it took. The road ahead would be long and difficult, but they would face it together.

For the rest of the meeting, they discussed the planning of the examinations, the timeline, and the coordination between all the specialists. There was a lot to plan and organize, but Danya felt a renewed sense of purpose. She had called this meeting for a reason, and now they had a clear path forward. It wouldn't be easy, but they were ready for whatever came next.

When the meeting finally adjourned, Danya stood at the front, looking at the group that had gathered to help her uncover the truth. They had committed themselves to this investigation, and now, they would follow through, no Matter what.

The mystery of Zayd's death wasn't over. And with the support of those around her, Danya knew that they were closer to finding the answers they needed.

Danya's Diary

It feels strange writing this down, but I need to get my thoughts on paper. So much has happened since we started this Journey, and I can't help but feel a mix of emotions. There's grief, confusion, but also a sense of determination. Every day brings us closer to the answers we need, but at the same time, I can't shake the feeling that there's so much more Beneath the surface that we're not seeing.

Today was one of those days where everything felt surreal. We had our meeting, and I tried to focus on the task at hand, but it's hard when your heart is heavy with so many thoughts. Zayd's death still feels so fresh. I can't believe he's really gone. Sometimes it feels like he's just out of reach, and any moment now, he'll walk through the door with one of his wise smiles or tell me to stop overthinking everything. But the truth is, he's gone, and we're left picking up the pieces.

I'm still in disbelief about how all of this unfolded. He was such a brilliant teacher, so full of life, and now, everything feels off balance. I see him in my memories, in all the little moments we shared together, both at home and with everyone he mentored. He taught me so much, not just in the professional sense, but about life itself. His insights were sharp, and his passion for knowledge was contagious.

What struck me the most in the meeting today was how everyone came together. I saw it in the faces of the historians trio—Naureen, Kanchana, and Elodie. They've been through a lot since we learned about Zayd's death. They were his students, and though they are strong, I can tell the weight of the loss has hit them hard. They were close to him, not just as his pupils, but as his friends. Seeing their faces, knowing they're with me in this, is the only thing that gives me comfort when I feel so lost in all of this.

They're the ones who helped me today, just like the ENT trio has always been there for me—Mira, Mia, and I, together. We've been through so much over the years, and I couldn't have asked for a better team to support me. Mira's strength, Mia's calmness, and my determination—those are the qualities that have helped us get this far. I can't imagine going through all of this without them.

And then there's the historians trio, who were also Zayd's students. They were by his side, learning from him, absorbing his lessons. Naureen, Kanchana, and Elodie—they have been my rock as well. It's like we're all bound together by the same thread, each of us with our own pain but with a shared purpose to uncover the truth about what happened to him.

It's hard not to feel the pressure sometimes, but the support I have around me helps me keep going. We all know that we're in this together, and that's what keeps me grounded. Every step we take, every piece of information we uncover, brings us closer to finding the answers. I know Zayd wouldn't want us to give up, and that's what drives me forward.

Today, as I sat in that meeting room, discussing all the plans we have for further examinations and investigations, I couldn't help but think back to our time in the past. All of us—Zayd included—sitting around, discussing cases, theories, and learning from one another. It was a time of collaboration, of pushing boundaries, and of striving for excellence. And even though Zayd isn't here now, his influence remains with all of us. His teachings are a part of us, and that will never change.

I also felt a sense of urgency today—like we're running out of time, even though we've come so far. The medical exams, the tests, the investigations... they're all crucial, but there's something about this case that doesn't sit right with me. I can't shake the feeling that we're being watched that someone doesn't want us to uncover the truth. But I won't let that stop us. We have to keep going, no Matter how difficult it gets.

As I left the meeting, I felt a quiet sense of determination building inside me. There's so much left to do, but I know we can do it. We have to. Not just for Zayd, but for ourselves, for the future. This is bigger than any one of us, and we all know it. But together, we'll see it through.

Tomorrow, we begin the next phase. The radiologists, the ENT specialists (us) and the rest of the team—we'll all continue to work together, step by step. Every test, every procedure, will bring us closer to the truth. I know it's not going to be easy, but I also know that we're ready for whatever comes next.

Zayd would have been proud of us. We're doing this for him. And for ourselves.

Chapter 17: The Examinations

The day was long, but everything went as planned. There was a sense of focused determination that filled the air as Danya, the ENT team, and the rest of the group carried out the necessary examinations. Each person had a specific role, and the flow of the day was meticulous, from the initial screenings to the more in-depth procedures. There was an air of quiet urgency, as if everyone knew how important these tests were in uncovering the truth about what happened to Zayd.

Danya had been deeply involved in every aspect of the examinations. She moved from one procedure to the next with an unshakable sense of purpose. She worked closely with the radiologists, Molly and Paula, to examine X-rays and scans, ensuring that all possible avenues were covered. Naureen, Kanchana, and Elodie had been invaluable too, supporting the process with their expertise. Their focus on the historical and medical context of the case, combined with their passion for Zayd's legacy, was a constant reminder of why they were all gathered here.

The ENT team had their own important tasks. Mira and Mia had been involved in performing nasoendoscope, while Danya worked alongside them in observing the intricate details that could provide vital clues. The three of them worked seamlessly, their years of collaboration evident in their flawless execution of each procedure.

The most important part of the day had been the laryngoscopies. Samira, Sara, and Elodie had taken charge of this. They'd been working carefully to understand any irregularities in the vocal cords and to look for any hidden signs that might not have been caught earlier. Everything was moving forward, with no unexpected hiccups. Every examination was thorough, and no detail was overlooked. It felt like a precise machine—a well-oiled system moving towards a common goal. And Danya could feel the weight of that goal pressing down on her, urging them to uncover the truth.

By late afternoon, most of the examinations had been completed, and the results were being compiled. There was a sense of quiet relief that began to fill the room. The data they had gathered was crucial, and it seemed like they were finally getting closer to a clearer picture of what had really happened.

But as the evening wore on, Danya's phone rang, breaking the calm that had settled over the group. She glanced at the screen, seeing the name of the hospital flashing in bold letters. Her heart skipped a beat—she knew what this meant. There was an emergency.

Her eyes flicked toward Nihal, who was sitting by her side. He gave her a knowing look, one that told her without words that he understood. The children were with Mira and Naureen, safe for the time being.

She excused herself from the group, stepping away to take the call in private. It was from the hospital's emergency department.

"Danya, we have two urgent cases," the voice on the other end said, clearly frantic. "One paediatric ENT surgery, and one adult case. Both are critical. We need you here immediately."

Danya's mind raced. She took a deep breath, collecting herself. "I'll be there as soon as I can," she said.

She ended the call, her mind already shifting gears. There was no time to waste.

Turning back to the group, she saw the concern on their faces. "I have to leave," she explained quickly. "There's an emergency at the hospital—two surgeries I need to attend to. A paediatric ENT case and an adult one. I'm sorry, but I need to go."

The team nodded, understanding without needing further explanation. They all knew that her work at the hospital was just as vital as their work in this investigation.

Naureen stepped forward. "Danya, you go. We'll handle things here. You've done enough today. Get to the hospital, and we'll take care of the rest."

Mira gave her a reassuring smile. "We'll keep working on the results. Don't worry about us. Go."

Danya's heart ached as she looked around at the group. She knew that they were counting on her, and she didn't want to leave them in the middle of such important work. But there was no choice. The hospital needed her.

She quickly gathered her things, excusing herself from the group. "I'll update you all as soon as I can," she promised. "I'm sorry I have to leave, but I know you'll keep moving forward with everything here."

Nihal stood up, his expression serious but supportive. "We'll be fine," he assured her, taking her hand in his before leaning in to kiss her cheek. "Do what you need to do. We'll be right here."

Danya gave him a quick nod, her heart heavy but resolute. She turned and left the meeting room, stepping into the hallway, heading toward the exit with a single goal in mind: the hospital.

As she walked, she tried to push the stress and the anxiety away, focusing instead on the task at hand. She knew that there was no time to waste. Every second counted in these critical surgeries, and she had to be prepared for whatever awaited her. The investigation would continue, but right now, her expertise was needed elsewhere.

The drive to the hospital was quick, though her mind remained occupied with the events of the day. She could still see the faces of her team, all working tirelessly to get to the bottom of the mystery.

She had to do her part. And right now, that part was in the operating room.

By the time she arrived at the hospital, the team was already prepping for the surgeries. Danya didn't hesitate. She immediately went to work, her hands steady as she reviewed the cases. The paediatric surgery was first—an emergency tonsillectomy that needed to be done immediately to prevent severe complications. The adult surgery was a complicated case involving a blocked airway that needed urgent intervention.

She worked methodically, guiding the team through the procedures, always focused, always steady. The surgeries went as planned, both patients stabilized. After what felt like hours, Danya finally stepped away from the operating table, her mind beginning to clear.

But as she took a breath, she couldn't help but think about the work that was still left to do with the investigation. She knew she had to go back. The team was counting on her. There were still so many unanswered questions.

With the surgeries complete, she quickly made her way back to her clinical room (located in the ENT area of the hospital) to update the team. There was no time to waste. The work was far from over.

Danya's Diary

It's been a whirlwind. Today, my holiday from work was officially over. I had to step back into the medical routine, back into the world I had been away from for too long. The transition was harder than I expected—especially with everything going on with Zayd and the investigation. But I guess there's no escaping the call of duty.

The day started with such promise. We had made so much progress with the examinations, and everything had been going smoothly. There was a sense of camaraderie in the air, the kind of teamwork that feels effortless because everyone knows exactly what they're doing. It almost felt like a pause in the storm—a brief moment of relief before the next wave.

But then the phone call came. The hospital needed me—urgently. Two critical surgeries. One paediatric ENT, one adult. I didn't even hesitate. I couldn't. There was no time to waste. I could see the worry in the eyes of my team as I explained I had to leave. I wanted to stay, to keep pushing forward with the investigation, but I couldn't ignore the hospital's need. I promised them I'd stay in touch, but deep down, I knew the priority had shifted, even if just for a while.

Nihal, always the steady presence, was supportive as usual. He didn't hesitate to encourage me to go. And, as always, the children were in good hands with Mira and Naureen. But there was a gnawing feeling as I left, like I was being pulled in two directions. The investigation was crucial, but so were my patients. I just hoped that the team would continue without me, that they wouldn't lose momentum.

The drive to the hospital was quick, my mind racing through the details of the surgeries. The paediatric tonsillectomy had to be done immediately, and the adult airway obstruction was no less urgent. The weight of both cases pressed heavily on me, but I had no choice but to push forward. I've done surgeries like these a hundred times, but today, everything felt sharper, more intense. It felt like everything was happening all at once—Zayd's death, the investigation, the patients, my responsibilities at the hospital.

When I arrived at the hospital, the team was already in motion. There was no time for pleasantries, no time to ease into the work. It was straight to business. And I was grateful for that. The paediatric surgery went smoothly—thankfully, it was a relatively simple procedure once we were in the operating room. The adult surgery, however, was a different story. A blocked airway is never a minor issue, and we had to act fast. The sense of urgency was palpable, but we made it through. Both patients were stable, and I allowed myself a brief moment of relief.

But even as I finished up, my mind was already racing back to the investigation. The questions about Zayd's death still loomed large, and I felt the weight of it all. I couldn't shake the feeling that we were on the verge of uncovering something—something important. It would only be a Matter of time.

I can't say I wasn't relieved when I was able to step away from the operating room and breathe again. But there's always a part of me that feels guilty when I'm not working, when I'm not helping. There's always a part of me that wonders if I'm missing something, if I could have done more, if I could have been there for everyone just a little longer.

But I couldn't stay at the hospital forever. I needed to check back in with the investigation, with the team. I made my way back to the office, eager to get back into the rhythm of things. There's so much to be done, and we're all so close. I feel it. We're getting closer to the truth, closer to understanding what really happened to Zayd. And that's what keeps me going. That's what I have to focus on right now.

Tomorrow will be another day, another step forward. For now, I'll rest—briefly, as usual. I just have to remind myself that I'm doing the best I can. I'll make sure my patients are taken care of, but I won't let the investigation slip through the cracks. We're in this together, and I'm not giving up. Not now. Not ever.

The road ahead is long, and there's still so much we don't know, but we're getting closer. I can feel it.

Tomorrow. Tomorrow, I'll dive back in—head first, heart full. I owe it to Zayd. To all of us.

Chapter 18: On Duty

Danya stood in her consulting room, listening intently as her patient, a middle-aged woman, described her ongoing hearing difficulties. The woman's voice trembled with a hint of concern as she described the sensation of fullness in her ears and the muffled sound she had been experiencing for weeks.

Danya looked at the patient, her expression calm but focused. She had seen cases like this before, and her experience told her that there was likely an underlying issue with the middle ear. However, she knew better than to make assumptions without a thorough examination.

"Let's take a closer look," Danya said, her voice soothing yet direct as she gently motioned for her patient to sit back in the examination chair. "I'm going to examine your ear with an otoscope first to check for any blockages or other issues that might be affecting your hearing."

The patient nodded, her eyes anxious, but trusting. Danya picked up the otoscope and positioned it at the entrance of the patient's ear canal. She carefully examined the ear, her trained eyes scanning for any signs of infection, fluid, or abnormal growths. The silence in the room was only broken by the faint hum of the otoscope and the quiet breathing of the patient.

After a moment, Danya pulled back and looked at the woman, a thoughtful frown on her face. "There's no infection here, but I'm noticing some fluid buildup behind the eardrum," she said, her voice steady. "That can sometimes lead to muffled hearing and the sensation of fullness. We'll need to do a bit more testing to confirm, but I think we may be dealing with something like otitis media. I'll schedule you for a hearing test, and we'll go from there."

The patient seemed relieved to have some answers, even if they weren't definitive yet. She nodded slowly, still processing the information.

"Don't worry," Danya added reassuringly. "We'll take care of this. I'll have the receptionist schedule your tests for you. In the meantime, I'll prescribe a decongestant to help reduce the fluid buildup. If it doesn't improve in the next few days, we'll explore other treatment options."

The patient smiled gratefully, and Danya offered her a warm, professional handshake before she left the room. As Danya took a moment to finish writing up the notes for the case, her phone buzzed. It was a message from Mira.

Mira:

Hey Danya, I was walking during my break and ended up talking to some oncologists in the hallway. They were discussing Zayd's case. Something's off... I'm not sure what, but they seem confused about something. I'll text you more in a bit.

Danya's heart skipped a beat as she read Mira's message. The confusion Mira had picked up on made her uneasy. The investigation into Zayd's death was always on her mind, but now, more than ever, something about it didn't feel right. She quickly typed a response.

Danya:

What exactly did they say? Are they questioning the diagnosis?

Mira replied almost immediately.

Mira:

Not exactly. They were talking about the progression of Zayd's cancer, and they seemed unsure about how quickly it had developed. I overheard one of them saying something about the "unusual speed" of it, but then they changed the subject quickly. I don't know... It just felt off. I'll text you everything they said.

Danya felt a chill run down her spine. She glanced at her watch. She had a few more patients to see before her break, but she couldn't shake the feeling that Mira had uncovered something important. Zayd's diagnosis had never sat right with Danya, but this new information—especially coming from oncologists—made her wonder if she was right to question everything.

She put her phone on silent and moved on to the next patient. The day continued on, but her thoughts remained with Mira's message, her mind running through all the possible scenarios. Could it be that Zayd's cancer wasn't as advanced as everyone had believed? Or was there something more to it? Something no one was seeing?

Meanwhile, Mira was finishing her walk and nearing the oncologists' office. She had been ruminating on their conversation, and as she crossed paths with them in the hallway again, she decided to take a chance. She approached one of the oncologists, a tall man in his mid-fifties, with silver hair and a serious demeanour.

"Excuse me," Mira said, trying to sound casual, though her voice carried a tone of concern. "I couldn't help but overhear your conversation earlier. You were talking about Dr. Zayd Hasan's cancer, right?"

The oncologist turned to her, a slight frown forming on his face, but he didn't appear surprised. It was clear from his response that he was used to questions.

"Yes," he replied, his voice measured. "We were discussing his case. We're all still trying to piece it together. His condition progressed much faster than what we would expect for a cancer of that type."

Mira's curiosity deepened. "But isn't that what you'd expect from late-stage cancer?"

The oncologist looked uncomfortable for a moment before he spoke again. "Yes, but... this doesn't quite fit the typical progression. It's hard to explain without going into the details, but there were certain things about his case that didn't add up. The speed of deterioration wasn't consistent with the diagnosis we had. That's all we'll say for now."

Mira pressed for more, but before she could ask another question, the oncologist quickly excused himself, as if regretting the conversation. Mira stood there for a moment, stunned, before she texted Danya, her fingers shaking slightly as she typed out the details.

Mira:

we were right. Something doesn't add up with Zayd's diagnosis. The oncologists were talking about how fast his cancer progressed, and they seemed confused about it. It wasn't what they expected from that kind of cancer. We need to dig deeper into this.

Danya's phone buzzed again, and she quickly read Mira's message. The words rang in her mind, but she knew she couldn't get distracted just yet. The investigation needed to continue, but now, more than ever, the pieces seemed to be falling into place. Zayd hadn't just died from cancer. He'd been the victim of something far more sinister.

Danya took a deep breath and prepared herself for the next patient. But this time, her mind wasn't entirely focused on her work. She was already planning the next steps in the investigation, knowing that the truth was out there, and they were getting closer to uncovering it.

Danya's Diary

Today was one of those days where everything feels like it's happening at once. The reality of returning to work after the break hit me harder than I expected. I've barely had time to breathe, let alone process everything that's happened in the last few weeks. Between the investigations into Zayd's death, the confusion surrounding his diagnosis, and all the ongoing medical work with my patients, it feels like I'm being pulled in a million directions.

The morning started off as usual with my consulting room filling up with patients. There was a middle-aged woman who came in complaining of muffled hearing and the sensation of fullness in her ear. It didn't seem too serious, but I could tell she was anxious. I examined her ear with the otoscope, and while there wasn't any infection, I noticed fluid behind the eardrum. I'm not surprised—it's a common issue, but I could see that the patient was worried. I reassured her and arranged a hearing test, telling her that we'd get to the bottom of it soon enough. There's always something so satisfying about helping someone with an issue that, while small, is so impactful on their daily life.

After that, the morning moved along with patients and paperwork. I had a moment to check my phone, and that's when I saw Mira's message. She'd overheard a conversation with some oncologists, and they were talking about Zayd's cancer. She mentioned that they were confused by the speed of its progression and how it didn't match the late-stage diagnosis they had. Of course, this immediately grabbed my attention. Zayd's death was never clear-cut in my mind, but hearing this from oncologists was unsettling. It's been eating at me ever since.

What if the cancer diagnosis was wrong? What if Zayd wasn't dying as quickly as they thought? Maybe, just maybe, there was something else going on that no one saw coming. And why would they have been so confident in his prognosis if the cancer wasn't what they expected? It feels like the closer we get to the truth, the more confusing it all becomes.

In the afternoon, Mira texted me again. She'd had more of a conversation with one of the oncologists, and apparently, they were still questioning the speed at which Zayd's condition deteriorated. From what she overheard, they were unsure if his cancer had progressed as quickly as it appeared. And they seemed to be uncomfortable even talking about it, which just raises more questions. Why would they be so hesitant? Was there something they didn't want to say?

I couldn't let this go. I know I've been busy with my patients, but Zayd was like family to me. He was a mentor, someone I trusted with my work. To think that his death might not have been as straightforward as we all thought... it feels wrong. I can't shake the feeling that we're being misled.

Meanwhile, work has been keeping me on my toes. My patient load is as busy as ever, and I've had to jump back into the medical routine faster than I'd like. I had to step back into the rhythm of surgeries, consultations, and emergencies, all while trying to keep my focus on Zayd's case. It's been a balancing act, and honestly, I'm exhausted.

Mira has been keeping me updated as she uncovers more pieces of the puzzle. Today, during her break, she overheard some unsettling conversations with the oncologists, and I can't help but think there's something bigger going on. I trust Mira, and if she's picking up on this, then there's definitely more to this than meets the eye.

As I sit here now, reflecting on everything, I can't help but wonder if I've missed something. What if there was something more to Zayd's case that we overlooked? What if those oncologists know something they're not saying? I've been so focused on helping my patients and doing my Job that I've allowed myself to drift from the deeper issue—what really happened to Zayd? I'm not sure I'll be able to rest until I get to the bottom of this.

Tomorrow, I have a busy day ahead. More patients, more surgeries, and more questions swirling in my mind. But Zayd's case is never far from my thoughts, and I'll do whatever it takes to figure out what really happened. I just hope that as we uncover the truth, we can bring some closure to everything.

I miss Zayd so much. His presence was a constant in my professional life. And now, all that remains is this aching feeling of uncertainty, and the desire to find answers. I can only hope that Mira and I can figure out what's really going on before it's too late.

I can feel the weight of the past few weeks on my shoulders, but I'm not giving up. Not now. Never in a million years.

Chapter 19: The Unexpected Knock on the Door

Danya had just wrapped up her last patient consultation for the day. The room was quiet now, the familiar hum of the hospital in the background. She sat back in her chair for a moment, staring at the case notes in front of her, but her mind was elsewhere. The past few days had been a whirlwind—between Zayd's sudden medical issues, Mira's unexpected conversation with the oncologists, and the ongoing concerns about the misdiagnosis. She felt a heavy weight pressing on her chest, a knot of unease she couldn't quite shake. Zayd, a man she'd worked alongside for years, was still in a coma, and every new piece of information seemed to raise more questions than answers.

Danya pushed the thoughts aside for a moment, focusing on the task at hand. She'd been busy, but there was always time for one more patient, one more case to solve. It was her routine, her life, and she had become accustomed to the constant ebb and flow of cases.

The room, as it always did, felt both familiar and strange. The soft light from the desk lamp cast shadows against the walls, and the sterile white of the room somehow made her feel more detached from the outside world. Yet the heavy feeling in her chest remained.

She was about to pick up her phone when a knock sounded at the consulting room door. It wasn't the usual knock, not one of her staff or colleagues—this knock was louder, more deliberate, and it made her jump slightly.

"Come in," Danya called, her voice calm but laced with a hint of curiosity. She set her phone down and looked up, waiting for the visitor to appear.

The door opened slowly, and two unfamiliar faces stepped into the room. Danya's eyes narrowed slightly as she took them in. They were both dressed in smart, professional attire—both in their mid-thirties, one man and one woman. They didn't look like patients, but they weren't staff either.

The man was tall, his posture straight, and he had short, dark hair that was neatly combed. His glasses reflected the light, making his eyes hard to read. The woman, slightly shorter, wore a soft expression but had an air of seriousness about her. She was glancing around the room as if assessing something, but Danya couldn't quite place what.

"Dr. Agarwal?" The man spoke first, his voice calm but with a sense of urgency. "We apologise for the intrusion, but may we have a moment of your time?"

Danya frowned, immediately sensing that something wasn't quite right. "Of course, but it's a bit late for a consultation. How can I help you?"

The woman spoke now, her voice polite but strained. "We're from the oncology department. Dr. Elizabeth Wilson, and this is Dr. Andrew Mitchell. We were hoping to speak with you regarding a Matter concerning Dr. Zayd Hasan."

At the mention of Zayd's name, Danya's stomach dropped. Zayd was still in a coma, his medical records muddled with confusion, and now these two were standing in front of her, clearly with something urgent on their minds. She motioned for them to sit down.

"Please, take a seat," Danya said, her mind racing. "What about Zayd? Is something wrong?"

Dr. Wilson and Dr. Mitchell exchanged a quick glance before the latter spoke up. "We've been reviewing Zayd's medical history in detail again, Dr. Agarwal. And we've come across something concerning."

"Concerning?" Danya repeated, her voice tight. "What do you mean by concerning? What's going on with his diagnosis?"

Dr. Wilson's face grew solemn. "We have reason to believe that the diagnosis he was given was incorrect. What we initially thought was late-stage cancer... it doesn't seem to match his symptoms."

Danya's heart skipped a beat. "Are you saying that Zayd didn't have late-stage cancer? That we've all been treating him for something he didn't have?"

Dr. Mitchell nodded grimly. "Exactly. After reviewing the scans again and considering the progression of his symptoms, we believe his cancer was much less advanced than we originally thought. What we've seen suggests that he had early-stage cancer—nothing close to the late-stage diagnosis we were led to believe."

Danya's mind raced. It felt impossible. She had been part of Zayd's care team for years, and his condition had always seemed dire. How could this have happened? How had they missed something so significant?

"What exactly are you saying?" Danya's voice was almost a whisper now. "How did this happen? How did we all miss it?"

Dr. Wilson's expression darkened, her eyes filled with a quiet frustration. "That's just it. We believe the diagnosis was manipulated. It wasn't just an oversight. There were people involved who misled us all. People who shouldn't have been part of the process in the first place."

Danya's heart pounded in her chest. "Who? Who were these people?"

Dr. Mitchell glanced at Dr. Wilson before speaking. "We believe two individuals—Alex and Anya Wong—who were acting as Zayd's oncologists, may not have been oncologists at all."

The shock hit Danya like a tidal wave. Alex and Anya Wong. She knew the names, had heard them mentioned in passing in the hospital corridors. They had been present during the early stages of Zayd's treatment, but Danya had always thought of them as qualified professionals. Now, it seemed like everything she had known had been turned upside down.

"Were they the ones acting as oncologists?" Danya asked, her voice barely audible. "What were they then? What were they doing?"

Dr. Wilson shook her head. "We don't have all the answers yet, but we suspect that they were using their position to manipulate not only Zayd's diagnosis but the entire medical team. They were involved in the decision-making process, but we now believe they weren't qualified at all."

The room seemed to close in on Danya. She had been a doctor for years, and to think that someone could fake their credentials and deceive an entire hospital felt unthinkable. And yet, here she was, sitting in front of two oncologists who were telling her that everything she thought she knew about Zayd's treatment might have been a lie.

"Why are you telling me this?" Danya asked, her voice shaking with a mixture of disbelief and anger. "Why come to me?"

Dr. Mitchell leaned forward slightly, his gaze intense. "We need your help, Dr. Agarwal. We've been reviewing Zayd's records, but we need someone who was close to him, someone who can help us uncover the truth. You've worked with Zayd for years, and we believe you can provide the missing pieces we need."

Danya's mind was spinning. She could barely process what they were telling her. Zayd had been a colleague, a friend. He had trusted these people, and now they were telling her that everything had been a lie.

"I'll help," Danya said, though her voice was steady. "But I need to know everything. I need to understand exactly what happened, who these people are, and what they've done."

Dr. Wilson nodded, her expression grateful. "We'll be in touch, Dr. Agarwal. We've just started digging into this, but we'll need your help to uncover the full story."

As they left, Danya stood in the middle of the room, her thoughts swirling. The pieces were starting to fall into place, but they raised even more questions. Zayd's case wasn't just a tragedy—it was a carefully orchestrated act of deception. And Danya was determined to find out the truth, no Matter where it led.

Danya's Diary

The past few days have been a blur. I'm still struggling to process everything that's happened, but I feel like I'm on the verge of something much bigger. Something that could completely change everything I've been working on for years. Today, I had a meeting with two oncologists—Dr. Elizabeth Wilson and Dr. Andrew Mitchell.

They came to my consulting room, unexpected and a little unsettling. It was so late in the day, and the knock on the door felt too deliberate, too sudden. I hadn't heard from either of them before, and as soon as they mentioned Zayd's name, I knew something wasn't right.

They told me they'd been reviewing Zayd's medical history again, and what they found was nothing short of alarming. It felt like a punch to the gut when Dr. Wilson said the words: "We believe the diagnosis he was given was incorrect." I didn't know what to think at first. Could this really be true?

Zayd had been diagnosed with late-stage cancer. Everyone, including me, had accepted it. The way his symptoms progressed, the scans we'd seen—it all pointed to a terminal diagnosis. But now, Dr. Wilson and Dr. Mitchell were telling me that it was a mistake. That the cancer was never in its late stage. It was early-stage cancer. How had I missed that? How had *we* all missed that?

And then came the real bombshell: they believed the diagnosis had been manipulated. Dr. Wilson and Dr. Mitchell were suggesting that Alex and Anya Wong, the oncologists who had been overseeing Zayd's treatment, might not even be oncologists at all. That they had somehow faked their credentials and misled the entire medical team, including me. The idea that I had been deceived by these people, trusted them with Zayd's care—it felt like the ground had been pulled out from under me.

I could hardly believe it. Alex and Anya were highly respected in the hospital, or so I thought. They'd been part of Zayd's early treatment, and yet now it seemed they had been manipulating the entire situation. How had they gotten away with it? What was their motive? And most importantly, what had happened to Zayd?

Dr. Wilson and Dr. Mitchell didn't have all the answers yet, but they were asking for my help to uncover the truth. They wanted me to dig deeper, to find the missing pieces that could expose the deception. I agreed, of course. I've worked with Zayd for years, and I owe it to him to find out what really happened. But I can't help but feel a sense of dread hanging over me. I have so many questions, but the answers I'm getting only lead to more uncertainty.

I haven't told anyone about this yet. I'm still processing it myself. But I know I can't keep it to myself for long. There are too many people involved, too many things at stake. I need to get to the bottom of this, for Zayd, for everyone who's been affected by this.

I just hope I can figure it out before it's too late.

Chapter 20: The Gathering

The afternoon sunlight filtered through the curtains of Danya's living room, casting a soft glow over the table set for tea. The familiar scent of chai filled the air, mingling with the quiet buzz of activity as Danya prepared for the afternoon gathering. She had invited Dr. Elizabeth Wilson and Dr. Andrew Mitchell, both seasoned doctors who had been crucial in the discovery of the truth about Zayd's diagnosis. It had been her idea to host this informal meeting in her home, a way to bring everyone together to discuss their next steps in a less clinical environment.

As she carefully arranged the cups and tea pots, Danya's thoughts wandered to the task at hand. They had come so far, but there was still so much to uncover. The revelation that Zayd's diagnosis had been fabricated had shaken her to the core, but it also gave her a renewed sense of purpose. She wasn't about to let this go. She was determined to get to the bottom of it all, and she knew she couldn't do it alone.

Mia, Mira, Naureen, Kanchana, and Elodie arrived first, their faces filled with both concern and determination. They greeted Danya with warm smiles, though there was an underlying seriousness to their expressions. They had all been on the same page for so long—working tirelessly to uncover the truth about Zayd. But now, it felt like they were on the precipice of something much bigger.

"Hey, Danya! Everything looks lovely," Mira said, her voice warm but tinged with the same unease Danya felt.

Danya smiled back but didn't respond right away. Instead, she gestured for everyone to take a seat. The room was filled with familiar faces, each one an integral part of the team. She glanced around the room, silently acknowledging the people who had stood by her through the entire ordeal.

"Thanks for coming, everyone," Danya said as she settled into a chair. "I know this situation is far from ideal, but we need to talk. There's a lot more at play than we initially thought."

Naureen nodded, folding her arms. "We're ready, Danya. What's the next step?"

Before Danya could respond, the doorbell rang. She stood quickly, walking to the door with a sense of anticipation. When she opened it, there stood Prekshya, the detective Danya had reached out to after everything that had transpired with Zayd. Prekshya had been a friend for years, someone Danya had trusted in difficult situations before. Her expertise in investigation would be invaluable.

"Prekshya, I'm glad you could make it," Danya said warmly, stepping aside to let her friend in.

"I wouldn't miss it," Prekshya replied with a small smile, her gaze flicking over the room. "I heard the situation's taken a turn."

Danya nodded, and they exchanged a brief but meaningful look before Prekshya joined the others.

With everyone now gathered, Danya finally took a deep breath and began to speak.

"Alright, I think it's time we all caught up," Danya started, her voice steady but filled with a quiet urgency. "Dr. Wilson and Dr. Mitchell have uncovered some troubling information. Zayd's diagnosis was completely wrong. What we were told about his late-stage cancer... it's not true. It was early-stage cancer if it even was cancer at all. The Wongs have been manipulating everything. And we need to understand why."

The room went silent as the team processed Danya's words. The shock was written across everyone's faces, but they didn't say anything. They all understood the gravity of the situation.

Dr. Wilson spoke up first. "Yes, we've confirmed that Zayd's diagnosis was misrepresented. But the more we dig into the Wongs, the more we realise they've been involved in something much bigger."

There was a long pause as everyone took this in. Danya could see the wheels turning in their minds, each of them trying to piece together the new information.

"What's their motive?" Kanchana asked, her brow furrowed in thought. "Why would they go so far to fake something like that?"

"I'm not sure," Danya replied, her voice low. "But that's why we need to work together. We can't let this go. We need to find the truth, no Matter what."

Mira leaned forward, her face serious. "If Zayd wasn't dying, then why did they try to kill him? We need answers, and we need them fast."

"I agree," Dr. Mitchell added, glancing at his colleagues. "We're not going to solve this if we don't act quickly. The Wongs are dangerous, and we don't know what they'll do next."

The conversation was cut short by the sound of the doorbell ringing once again. Danya stood, her pulse quickening as she made her way to the door. This time, it was Mia, one of her closest friends and a member of the ENT team, who stepped inside.

"Sorry I'm late," Mia said with a small smile. "The clinic was running over. What did I miss?"

"You're right on time," Danya replied, gesturing to the group. "We're just getting started."

Mia nodded and made her way to the table, sitting down with the others. The ENT team, which included Mira, Danya, and Mia, had worked closely together for years. Their bond was unbreakable, and Danya knew they were going to need all their collective expertise to unravel the mystery surrounding Zayd's case.

"I've been thinking about everything," Mia said, her voice calm but full of concern. "If the Wongs were involved in something this extreme, then they have resources. They've been hiding something for a long time."

"That's why we need to dig deeper," Prekshya added. "And that's where I come in. I'll start looking into their financials and any other connections they might have."

Danya nodded, grateful for her friend's willingness to help. "Thank you, Prekshya. We need all the help we can get."

As the afternoon wore on, the group discussed their next steps. There was a lot to do, and everyone had a role to play. They all agreed to keep things quiet for now, to gather as much information as possible before making any moves. Danya had never felt more connected to her team—her friends. They were in this together, and together, they would get to the bottom of it all.

Before they parted ways, Danya looked around at the faces of her colleagues and friends, their expressions a mix of determination and concern.

"Thank you all for coming," she said, her voice thick with emotion. "We're going to figure this out, one step at a time."

The team nodded in agreement, knowing that whatever came next, they would face it together.

As the last of her guests left, Danya couldn't help but feel a renewed sense of purpose. With the support of her colleagues, the truth about Zayd's case was within reach. They would uncover what had really happened, and no Matter what it took, they would make sure justice was served.

Danya's Diary

The house feels quiet now that everyone has left, but my mind is anything but still. I can't stop thinking about today's gathering. It was supposed to be just a casual tea, a moment of respite after everything we've been through. Yet somehow, even in the warmth of my living room, surrounded by friends and colleagues, the shadow of Zayd's case loomed large.

I couldn't help but notice how natural it felt to have everyone together. The ENT trio—Mira, Mia, and me—has always been close. Ever since our student days under Zayd's mentorship, the three of us have been inseparable. Zayd was more than just a teacher to us; he was our guide, our inspiration. He taught us not only how to diagnose and treat but also how to think critically and act with compassion.

Sitting across from us today were the history trio—Kanchana, Naureen, and Elodie. They too were Zayd's students, and I could see the same spark of determination in their eyes that he used to ignite in all of us. It's strange how our paths, though so different, all seem to lead back to him. Kanchana's sharp intellect, Naureen's calm resolve, Elodie's unshakable focus—all of it traces back to Zayd.

Naureen, especially, has a presence that anchors everyone around him. He was quiet today, listening more than speaking, but when he did speak, it was with the weight of someone who has spent sleepless nights turning over every detail in his mind. I think we're all like that now—restless, unable to settle until we've uncovered the truth.

Mia, Mira, and I couldn't stop talking after everyone left. It's always been like that with us, hasn't it? We can debate endlessly, challenge each other, and still leave the conversation feeling closer than ever. Today was no exception. We went over every piece of information we've gathered, every theory we've considered. And still, nothing feels certain.

Zayd's presence feels so strong in moments like these. I can almost hear him guiding us, nudging us to look deeper, to ask better questions. It's strange to think about how much of who I am today was shaped by him. He had this way of making you feel like you could do anything, as long as you approached it with thoughtfulness and care.

And now, to know that he's not truly gone, that he's out there somewhere, fighting to wake up from this nightmare—it's overwhelming. The thought keeps me awake at night. How could anyone do this to him? To someone who gave so much to the world?

I saw the same anger and confusion reflected in Mira's and Mia's eyes today. We didn't need to say it aloud; we all feel it. It's not just about uncovering the truth for Zayd's sake—it's about standing up for everything he stood for.

The history trio is just as invested. Kanchana, with her methodical approach, has been piecing together every lead we have. Elodie, with her keen memory, has been poring over every document, every detail. And Naureen—his quiet but steady presence has kept us all grounded.

I keep replaying the moment Prekshya walked through my door today. Seeing her reminded me of all the times we've leaned on each other in difficult moments. She's brilliant, intuitive, and, more importantly, someone I trust completely. With her help, I feel like we have a real chance of getting to the bottom of this.

Still, there's so much we don't know. So many loose threads. The Wongs, their motive, the fabricated diagnosis—it's all swirling in my mind like a puzzle with too many missing pieces.

And then there's the oncologists, Dr. Wilson and Dr. Mitchell. They've been incredible, but even their expertise hasn't been enough to untangle this web completely. I can't help but wonder if we're missing something obvious, something right in front of us.

As I sit here now, writing this, I'm struck by how interconnected we all are. Zayd brought us together, not just as students, but as a family. Even in his absence, he's the glue holding us together, driving us forward.

I know the road ahead won't be easy. There are still so many questions, so many obstacles. But if there's one thing I'm certain of, it's that we won't give up. Mira, Mia, Naureen, Kanchana, Elodie, and I—we owe it to Zayd, to ourselves, to see this through.

And we will. Together.

Chapter 21: Investigation

Danya had just finished a long shift in the A&E ward, but there was little time to rest. Her watch showed that she had 45 minutes before she had to prepare for two surgeries—one a routine tonsillectomy and the other an experimental procedure she'd developed herself for tinnitus. But there was a pressing issue at hand that couldn't wait.

She stood in the corridor of the hospital, still in her black scrubs and white coat, with a baby pink surgical cap perched atop her head. Her scrubs were a symbol of her position as head of the ENT department, though today, the weight of that role seemed particularly heavy. The long hours and chaotic moments in the A&E ward had taken their toll, and she felt every bit of exhaustion in her bones. But she couldn't ignore the unease creeping in about the investigation into the fake CVs and the footage that had been circulating.

Danya walked into the HR office first, her footsteps echoing in the empty hallway as she passed other staff members who were focused on their own busy work. When she entered the HR manager's office, the warm, neutral-toned walls did little to soothe the storm brewing inside her.

"Dr. Agarwal, you're here," said Emma, the HR manager. "I hope everything's alright. You look like you've had a full day already."

Danya smiled tiredly. "It's been... one of those days. I just got out of A&E. Had to see a five-year-old who had a stone stuck in her ear, a seven-year-old with severe quinsy from tonsillitis, and a four-year-old who managed to swallow a hairclip." Her voice was a mix of exhaustion and disbelief. "It's shocking, to be honest. So, yeah, I'm not exactly at my best right now."

Emma looked concerned, her eyebrows furrowing as she leaned forward. "That sounds intense. Are you okay?"

"I'm fine," Danya replied, though the weariness in her voice gave her away. "Just a bit... overwhelmed, I guess. But there's no time to waste. We need to focus on the issue at hand—the fake CVs and the footage."

She moved toward the desk, her coat swishing as she did, the fabric of her black scrubs hidden Beneath it. Emma gave a nod, signalling for her to sit. "Of course, Dr. Agarwal. Let's get to it."

"I need to know exactly who processed those CVs. Do we have any trace of where they came from? Any department, any staff member who might have had access to them?"

Emma tapped on her keyboard and brought up a file on the computer screen. "I've been going through the HR records. As you know, it's been hard to pinpoint exactly where the fake CVs came from, but we have a few suspects. It looks like they were processed through multiple departments before they got to us—so the trail is a bit muddled."

Danya sighed, her mind racing. "We need more concrete evidence. We can't afford any more mistakes. If we don't get this sorted, people could lose their Jobs, or worse, their careers."

Emma nodded. "I agree. I'll keep digging into it, and I'll make sure everything's logged properly. But if you have any other leads or ideas, feel free to share."

"Thanks, Emma. Please keep me updated," Danya said, getting up. She had to be quick—she couldn't afford to lose any more time.

Next, she walked down the corridor toward the IT department. The digital side of the investigation was just as vital. The footage of the questionable interactions had raised red flags, and it was crucial to understand how and why it had been altered in the first place. Danya entered the IT office, where Sam, the head of the department, was hunched over a computer.

"Dr. Agarwal!" he greeted her with a surprised glance, pushing his glasses up his nose. "What brings you here?"

"I need your help," Danya said quickly, sitting down on the chair opposite him. "I need to see the full records of the footage that's been tampered with. I know you've been looking into it, but I need to understand how it happened."

Sam turned toward her, his expression suddenly serious. "I've been working on this, and it's strange. There's evidence that someone edited the timestamps and altered the content in the footage. The changes are subtle, but they're there. We'll need to trace the source of these edits."

Danya rubbed her temple, feeling the stress building up. "Is there anything you can tell me about who had access to the footage? I know that kind of thing is usually limited, but we've got to narrow it down."

"We're still working on tracking down who had direct access," Sam replied, scrolling through his computer screen. "But we did identify one individual who's been involved in multiple log-ins. It's all pointing to someone within the hospital, possibly someone who has access to both the video systems and the HR database."

Danya's mind was already turning. She needed to keep her focus sharp. "We need to move fast. If we don't get to the bottom of this quickly, it could affect everything we've worked for."

Sam nodded. "Agreed. I'll keep working on this, and we'll set up a meeting with the security team to run a full audit. We can't let this go unnoticed."

"Thank you, Sam. Please keep me updated immediately if you find anything new," Danya said, standing up. Her hands were trembling slightly from the adrenaline that coursed through her.

The clock was ticking, and every moment felt more urgent. Her surgeries were drawing closer, but there was a fire burning inside her to uncover the truth.

She took a deep breath and forced herself to refocus. The two surgeries she was about to perform would require all her skill and concentration. But this case, the fake CVs, the footage—it was becoming too much of a distraction. She couldn't afford to let it cloud her mind during the delicate procedures she was about to undertake.

As she stepped back into the corridor, her mind still racing, Danya felt a flicker of hope. The pieces of the puzzle were starting to fall into place, even if she couldn't see the full picture yet. With the HR team, the IT department, and everyone else working tirelessly, she was confident that they'd get to the bottom of this—and soon.

But for now, there was work to do. And in 45 minutes, she had to be ready to go into the operating theatre once again.

Danya's Diary

The tinnitus surgery went smoothly today, although it was more time-consuming than I had expected. It's a procedure I developed myself, and even though I've done it several times now, I always feel a mix of excitement and anxiety before performing it. Today, it was just another case that went off without a hitch, though I can't help but notice how draining it can be to focus so intensely for that long. It's rewarding, but it does take a lot out of me.

Before that, I performed a routine tonsillectomy, which felt almost like a break in comparison. It's always a little less stressful when you're dealing with something familiar, but even so, no surgery is ever entirely without pressure. I'm always mindful of my patients, especially in cases like that. A tonsillectomy might seem simple, but it still requires a great deal of attention to detail, particularly when it comes to ensuring there are no complications. Thankfully, that went well too, and the patient is doing fine.

As soon as I finished the surgeries, I had only a short window to collect myself before my rounds in the ward. It's strange to think that something as taxing as surgery can almost feel like a break when I know what lies ahead in the ward. The pace never slows down. But I'll take a moment to gather myself before heading out. At least I can take comfort in knowing that those surgeries went well. There was a certain peace in the success of both procedures.

I've also been pushing myself to stay on top of everything that's happening with the investigation into the fake CVs and the footage. My meeting with Sam, the IT manager, didn't reveal much more than what we already knew. The situation is complicated, and it feels like it's going to take longer than I anticipated to dig deeper into the truth. Sam's team is doing their best, but every answer leads to another question, and I'm trying not to let the stress interfere with my day-to-day work.

The HR department is still working on it, and I've asked them to keep me updated regularly. Honestly, it's hard to think about anything else when I know how much is riding on this investigation. It feels like there are so many moving parts, and I can't shake the feeling that we're getting closer to uncovering something big.

But for now, I need to put that out of my mind. There are patients to check on and a busy day ahead. The ward won't wait, and neither will the next surgery I need to prepare for. I just need to take one step at a time. Right now, that means getting through these rounds and making sure my patients are well taken care of.

Chapter 22: The Turnaround

The rumours were spreading like wildfire across the hospital. It seemed that everywhere Danya went—whether it was the Green Zone, where the ENT department was, or the Teal Zone, where oncology worked—the whispers about the Wongs were everywhere. People were talking, speculating, and sharing their theories. And the stories were all the same: the Wongs were frauds, impostors who had managed to fool everyone into believing they were legitimate oncologists. They had even gone so far as to lie about their credentials, pretending to be highly regarded professionals in a field they knew nothing about.

Danya's mind raced as she walked through the hallways of the hospital. She had just finished her rounds in the ward and was heading back to her office when she overheard a nurse from the oncology department talking to a colleague. "I heard they never even worked in oncology," the nurse was saying. "Their whole CV was fake. They just wanted to get close to Zayd."

Danya's heart sank. She had heard the same thing from Mia and Mira earlier. The Wongs' names had been circulating all over the hospital, and the stories about them only seemed to grow more unsettling the longer they were discussed. The more they dug, the more it became clear that Alex and Anya Wong were impostors, not oncologists. Danya's thoughts were racing. How had they managed to fool everyone? How had they gotten away with it for so long? And more importantly—why? What was their end game?

Her steps quickened as she made her way to the office. She found Mia and Mira already there, poring over the files they had gathered. "Any updates?" Danya asked, her voice low as she stepped into the room.

Mia looked up from her computer screen, her brow furrowed. "It's worse than we thought," she said quietly. "We've dug into their backgrounds, and everything checks out to a point, but there's something off about their history. It's all fake. Their qualifications, their work experience, even their hospital affiliations... they're not real."

Mira nodded, still scanning the information on her tablet. "And the part that really stands out? They seemed to have specifically targeted Zayd. I don't know how, but they were close to him—closer than anyone should have been with their credentials. We're still trying to figure out exactly how they managed that."

Danya sighed deeply, running a hand through her hair. The weight of the situation was starting to press down on her. The fact that these people had infiltrated the hospital under false pretences was disturbing enough, but the idea that they had somehow been involved in Zayd's situation was what kept her up at night. Zayd had been more than a colleague to them—he had been a mentor, a friend. The idea that someone had deliberately put him in harm's way was unimaginable.

"What about Zayd?" Danya asked, her voice tight. "Have we learned anything about his condition? Is there any hope for him? We need to start thinking about how we're going to bring him back."

Mia and Mira exchanged looks, their expressions grim. "We've been discussing it," Mia said softly. "We can't give up on him. But it's complicated. Zayd's been in a coma for so long. The doctors say there's not much hope, but we know him. We know what he's capable of. And we believe he'll wake up."

Danya's heart raced. "So, what do we do now?"

Mira tapped the screen of her tablet, bringing up the latest scans of Zayd's brain activity. "We're going to have to push the boundaries of medicine," she said. "We have to try everything we can to stimulate his brain. Maybe there's something we're missing. If anyone can figure it out, it's us."

Danya looked at her two closest colleagues, the people she trusted more than anyone else. They had been through a lot together. They had faced challenges, both personal and professional, but they had always been able to overcome them as a team. This time would be no different.

"Let's get to work," Danya said, determination in her voice. "We can't let these frauds get away with this, and we can't let Zayd slip away either."

Mia and Mira nodded in agreement. It was time to turn the tide.

As the hours passed, Danya found herself back in the Green Zone, reviewing the medical records of Zayd and the Wongs. The investigation into their backgrounds was taking up every bit of her attention. She couldn't shake the feeling that there was more to the story. She could feel it in her gut. They weren't just frauds—they were dangerous, and they had managed to manipulate the entire situation, including Zayd.

But they wouldn't get away with it. Not on her watch.

And as for Zayd, well, they wouldn't give up on him. Not yet.

Danya's team, her family, her closest colleagues—together, they would uncover the truth and make sure that Zayd had the chance he deserved. It was just a Matter of time.

She looked at the files one last time before heading to the surgery room. There was work to do, and she wouldn't rest until the truth came out.

The turnaround had begun.

Danya's Diary

It's been a long few days, but we're finally starting to get somewhere. The investigation into the Wongs has been a whirlwind, and it's exhausting trying to keep up with all the information and all the rumours swirling around. Honestly, the whole thing has been incredibly overwhelming. The more we dig, the more shocking it gets. I keep reminding myself that we have to stay focused—Zayd needs us.

Mira, Mia and I have been going through everything, trying to make sense of the Wongs' backgrounds. It's like they were playing a game, and we were the pawns. They managed to manipulate everyone around them, but the cracks are starting to show. We've found discrepancies in their CVs, their work histories, and even in the hospital affiliations they claimed to have. They've been pretending to be oncologists all this time, and no one saw through it.

The hardest part of all this is knowing how involved they were in Zayd's case. It just doesn't make sense. How did they manage to get so close to him? How did they get into the position they were in? I can't stop asking myself these questions, but right now, there's no clear answer.

On top of all of this, we can't give up on Zayd. I know we're all thinking about him constantly. Mira and Mia have been working with me to produce a plan to bring him back. Everyone keeps saying there's no hope, but I don't believe that. Not for a second. Zayd is strong, and we've all seen him fight through challenges before. He won't just give up. We can't give up on him either.

The plan is to keep pushing. Push the boundaries, try new things, and get to the bottom of the mess the Wongs have created. We've already made some progress in gathering information, but it's just the beginning. I know we have a long way to go before we uncover the whole truth.

There's something about all of this that doesn't sit right with me, though. I keep thinking about what the oncologists said—the ones who helped Zayd before everything fell apart. Why didn't anyone question the Wongs sooner? How did they manage to fool everyone for so long?

I know we'll figure it out eventually. It's just going to take time, and right now, time isn't on our side. I'm hoping that when the truth finally comes out, we'll be able to find a way to save Zayd. I can't stand the thought of losing him. He's been more than a mentor—he's been a friend.

For now, we keep digging. We keep looking for answers, and we keep pushing for Zayd. I'm not going to rest until we get to the bottom of this, and I won't stop until I know Zayd is safe and on his way to recovery.

Time is ticking, and the investigation is only just beginning.

Chapter 23: The Results

The results were finally in, and everything we had suspected, everything we had feared, was coming to light. The team had been working around the clock, running tests, checking records, and piecing together the fragments of the mystery that surrounded Zayd's sudden collapse. Every person who had been part of his care team had left no stone unturned. Danya, Mia, and Mira—together with Dr. Elizabeth Wilson, Dr. Andrew Mitchell, and a handful of other specialists—had reviewed every single detail of Zayd's medical history, his last moments in the hospital, and the strange circumstances leading to his "death."

We had to be thorough. Zayd's life was at stake, and no one, not a single one of us, could afford to miss something critical. For hours, we poured over the toxicology reports, checked and rechecked every possible source of contamination or poisoning. The results were inconclusive at first. The blood tests, scans, and everything in between didn't give us the answers for which we were hoping. We were all tired, drained, and desperate, but we kept going, determined to find out what had really happened to him.

And then, we found it.

Zayd had been poisoned. There were toxins in his system—dangerous, debilitating chemicals—that had rendered him unconscious and placed him in a coma. It was chilling to think about how they had gone unnoticed until now. It explained everything. The strange symptoms, the sudden collapse, the hospital's initial confusion—it was all beginning to make sense.

Laila, Zayd's sister, had been by his side since the very beginning, trying to understand what had happened to her brother. When she and Evelyn, Zayd's wife, found out about the toxins, the shock was palpable. Evelyn's reaction was one of disbelief at first, her hands shaking as she tried to process the information. But Laila, ever the protector, was focused. There was no time for disbelief; she had to know the truth, and she was ready to do anything to help her brother.

Zayd's oldest child, Samira, a paediatrician herself, had heard the commotion from the Blue Area, the paediatrics wing. It was half-term, and Sara, her younger sister, was spending the day with her. It seemed like just another day, but when Samira and Sara heard the hushed voices and the hurried footsteps, they knew something wasn't right. The two of them made their way to the source of the commotion, following the trail of concerned voices. Samira was one of the first to learn about the toxins, the poisons that had been lurking in her father's system.

Sara, ever the curious one, was with her sister when the news broke. Samira, her face pale but composed, explained as best as she could what had happened. The conversation was difficult for Sara to fully understand—she was young, after all—but Samira did her best to assure her that they were all working to save their father.

The whole team was in the room when the full scope of the situation became clear. Everyone felt the weight of the discovery. There was no denying it now—Zayd had been deliberately poisoned. But by who? Why?

At that moment, it felt like the world had shifted Beneath us. We had always suspected foul play, but now we knew for sure that Zayd had been the victim of a malicious act. The toxins in his system had caused the coma, but who had administered them? And how had they gone undetected for so long?

The next steps were critical. We needed to focus on getting Zayd out of this coma. We also needed to make sure that no one else was exposed to the same fate. It was clear now that there were dangerous forces at play, and we couldn't afford to wait around. The investigation had just taken a sharp turn.

We still had more questions than answers, but one thing was clear: Zayd wasn't just a casualty in a medical mystery—he was the victim of an attack. And now, we would do everything in our power to ensure he would pull through and that justice would be served.

The fight was far from over.

Danya's Diary

The weight of everything that's happened today feels almost unbearable. The truth is finally out, but it's far worse than I could have ever imagined. It wasn't just an accident, or an unexplained illness, or some rare complication. No. Zayd was poisoned. The Wongs—Alex and Anya—had put dangerous toxins into some of his medication. The whole team has been working tirelessly to piece this together, and it's beyond unsettling.

I can't believe it. I've known Zayd for years. He's been a mentor, a colleague, a friend. To think that someone could deliberately harm him like this...it's beyond comprehension. What was their goal? To get rid of him? To ruin him? I don't know what their motives were, but I feel a sense of betrayal that cuts so deeply. They had worked so hard to gain his trust, to get close to him, and now we see what they were really capable of.

Mira, Mia, and I were in the thick of things today. We've been following leads, going over his medical records, and examining the medications he was prescribed. It was Mia who found the connection first. There was something off about a specific batch of the drugs that Zayd had been taking. After checking the pharmacy records and running some tests on the pills, we found traces of a toxin. A slow-acting poison that would have put him into a coma, exactly how it had played out.

The rest of the team is shaken, but we're focused. Zayd is in a coma, but now at least we have a clear picture of what happened. The Wongs—Alex and Anya—must have used their positions to gain access to his prescriptions, adding something lethal to his medication. I still can't fathom how they pulled it off. I had no idea they were capable of something like this. For all we knew, they were respected oncologists. But it was all a lie. Their entire professional façade was a carefully constructed mask.

I had to sit down with Laila and Evelyn today. Zayd's sister and wife are devastated, as you would expect. Laila, especially, has been a rock through all of this, but I can see the worry in her eyes. She's holding it together, but I know it's hard for her to process. And Evelyn…she's in a state of disbelief. She trusted them too, and now this. It's just too much for anyone to take in.

Samira, their eldest child, overheard us talking about the toxins from the Blue Area. She and her younger sister, Sara, had been spending time at the hospital today. Samira had to hear it from us first. It was awful to see the shock on her face, but she's a strong woman. I know she's going to help her family through this. Sara, though, poor thing. She's too young to really understand, but Samira did her best to explain.

The entire team is feeling this. Zayd wasn't just a colleague; he was our friend. We've all been affected by this, and I know that we'll work relentlessly to make sure he pulls through. But the feeling of betrayal, the sense of being violated—it's hard to shake. I'm trying to focus on the next steps, but it's difficult. We need to make sure Zayd recovers and that justice is served.

The Wongs might have thought they were clever, but they underestimated us. We're not going to let this go. Not while Zayd's still fighting. And we'll make sure they pay for what they've done. I don't care how long it takes. This isn't just about Zayd's recovery anymore; it's about making sure they never hurt anyone else.

I don't know what's going to happen in the days ahead, but I won't stop. We won't stop. This is just the beginning.

Chapter 24: The Revival

The tension in the operating room was palpable. It wasn't just the weight of the surgery that hung in the air—it was the culmination of everything that had led to this moment. The threat of the poisoning, the shock of discovering early-stage laryngeal cancer, the weight of Zayd's condition, and the lingering questions surrounding his situation all built to this point. Everyone was aware that this surgery could be the turning point, not only for Zayd's health but for the future that lay ahead for all of them.

Danya, Mia, and Mira had been working together for hours, preparing for the operation. They had run through the details repeatedly, double-checking the strategy. The stakes were high—every move Mattered. Zayd's body had been under immense strain from the toxins he had been exposed to, and the cancer was still an additional factor they hadn't anticipated. But there was hope now.

The decision was made to perform a functional endoscopic surgery, a method that would allow them to remove the early-stage cancerous tissue from Zayd's larynx without causing too much disruption to the surrounding structures. It wasn't a simple procedure, but it was the best option. The goal was clear: remove the cancer while giving Zayd a chance to recover from the poison that had nearly taken his life.

As the team got ready, Danya stood next to Zayd in the preparation area. The anaesthesiologist was administering the sedatives, and Danya couldn't help but look at her mentor, her colleague, and her friend. His body lay still, but his presence loomed large. Zayd had always been someone who faced challenges head-on, never backing down from adversity. She couldn't let herself feel the weight of the situation too much—this was their time to act, and they had to get it right.

"Zayd," Danya whispered, her voice almost breaking. "We're going to get you through this. Stay strong. We've got you."

The surgery began after Zayd was properly sedated, and they all moved into position. Mia, who had been working alongside Danya for years, was ready to assist with the endoscopic procedure. Mira, ever the vigilant one, kept an eye on Zayd's vital signs. The operating room was methodical, almost serene in its controlled chaos. Every step had to be precise. Any mistake would mean setbacks they couldn't afford.

Danya and Mia worked in sync, carefully navigating the endoscope through Zayd's larynx, inspecting the area for the cancerous tissue. The surgery itself was time-consuming, each movement deliberate and calculated, but it was necessary. Zayd's laryngeal cancer was still in its early stages, but it had spread enough that they needed to remove it entirely to avoid complications in the future. They worked with precision, making sure not to damage any of the surrounding tissues, especially since the toxins still lingered in his system.

Mira's voice cut through the room at regular intervals, offering observations on Zayd's condition. "Heart rate steady. Oxygen levels normal. Keep moving, team. We're making progress."

With every passing minute, the sense of urgency waned, and the focus on the task at hand took precedence. Zayd's condition was critical, but they couldn't afford to rush the operation. Mia and Danya continued to remove the cancerous cells with steady hands, while Mira kept checking Zayd's vitals and noting any changes. As time passed, the initial panic started to fade into a sense of calm determination. This was their moment, and they had to make it count.

The laryngeal cancer was successfully removed. It was a difficult procedure, but they had done it. They'd removed the dangerous cells that had threatened Zayd's health, and they had done so without compromising the function of his voice box. The hope was that, with proper treatment, Zayd would wake up and start recovering soon.

The team was tired, their energy spent, but there was a feeling of accomplishment in the air. This was a huge victory. But it wasn't over. Zayd was still in a coma, still fighting the poison in his system, and they couldn't rest yet. They had done everything they could for his cancer, but his recovery from the toxins was still uncertain.

As they completed the surgery, Danya stood for a moment by the operating table, breathing deeply, trying to collect her thoughts. She could feel the exhaustion in every inch of her body, but she couldn't stop now. Zayd needed them. She took one final glance at him before they moved him to the recovery area.

The surgical team went over everything once more, making sure they had done everything correctly. "It's done," Mia said, looking at Danya with a weary smile.

"For now," Danya replied, her voice calm but firm. "We still need to keep him stable. He's not out of the woods yet."

The recovery room was quiet, with only the hum of the machines monitoring Zayd's vital signs. Nurses moved efficiently, keeping a close eye on him, while Danya, Mia, and Mira lingered nearby, watching over him. They couldn't leave yet—not until they were certain that he was stable. Zayd's recovery would take time, but at least they had given him a chance.

Danya couldn't help but feel a sense of relief wash over her. This had been their best shot at saving him, and she was determined to see it through. Zayd had been a mentor, a colleague, and a friend, and she wasn't about to let him slip away.

Mia stood beside her, looking at Zayd with a mix of hope and exhaustion. "We've done what we can for now," Mia said softly. "Let's just hope he pulls through."

Mira nodded, her expression serious. "We'll be here when he wakes up. He's not alone."

Danya glanced at the two of them, grateful for their support. She had always known that she could count on them, and this was no different. They had been through so much together, and now, as a team, they had saved Zayd's life.

"We've got this," Danya murmured, more to herself than to anyone else. "He's going to make it."

As they moved out of the recovery room, Danya's phone buzzed. It was a text from Samira. "How's he doing?" it read.

Danya typed back quickly. "We did it. Surgery's over. He's stable for now."

She paused, staring at the screen for a moment. There was still so much to do—more surgeries, more recovery, more tests. But for now, they had done everything they could. The rest would depend on Zayd's strength and his will to fight.

The road ahead was uncertain, but one thing was clear: they weren't giving up. Not now. Not ever. Zayd was going to make it through this. And they were all going to be there when he did.

Danya's Diary

I only have two minutes before my next surgery, but I needed to check on Zayd. I can't help but feel relieved that the surgery went well. He's stable for now, but I know it's still a waiting game. I can't let my guard down. Mia and Mira are by his side, keeping watch. They're all I can trust right now.

I hate that I can't be there longer, but my duty calls. I just hope he stays strong. He's been through so much, but I know Zayd. He'll fight. He always does.

Chapter 25: The Reunion

The recovery room was quiet, the steady hum of machines in the background providing a rhythmic reminder of the fragile state Zayd was in. Danya stood at the doorway for a moment, taking in the sight of her old mentor, lying unconscious but stable on the bed. It was a relief to see him awake after everything that had happened, but Danya knew the Journey ahead would still be long.

Mia and Mira had stayed by his side throughout the night, ensuring that all his vital signs remained stable. As Danya entered, they both looked up, their tired eyes filled with cautious optimism.

"He's stable," Mia said, her voice soft. "Still unresponsive, but he's making progress."

Danya nodded, her gaze drifting over to Zayd's still form. "I'll call the others in," she said, turning to head toward the door.

She pulled out her phone and quickly dialled the numbers of the History Trio: Naureen, Kanchana, and Elodie. They had been anxious to see Zayd, just as she had. It was time to bring them in—they had all been part of this Journey, and now, they could finally witness the moment they had all been waiting for.

Within minutes, the History Trio arrived, looking both excited and nervous. The group, though varied in their specialties, shared a bond with Zayd that went beyond just their professional lives. They were like family, and this moment meant everything to them.

Naureen, Kanchana, and Elodie entered the room, their faces lighting up as they saw Zayd. He was pale, hooked up to various machines, but he was alive, and that was the most important thing.

"Is he—?" Elodie asked, her voice trembling with emotion.

"He's stable, but still not fully conscious," Danya explained, stepping aside to let them approach the bed. "We've made progress, but it's going to take time."

Zayd's eyes flickered open slowly, and for a moment, he seemed disoriented. Then, his gaze cleared, and a small, strained smile appeared on his lips. "I see everyone is here," he said hoarsely, his voice weak but familiar.

Danya felt a surge of relief at hearing his voice. It was Zayd, there was no mistaking it.

"Zayd!" Everyone in the room exclaimed, her voice full of relief. "You're awake."

"Dad! I can't believe you are alive!" Sara and Samira blurted with excitement.

"I knew my Uncle could be saved!" Omar and Rami squealed in unison.

"Of course I'm awake," he replied with a weak chuckle. "Couldn't let you all have all the fun without me, could I?"

The group gathered around him, each one offering a comforting presence. They had all been through so much, and now, they could share this moment together. Zayd's eyes scanned each of them, landing last on Danya.

"How's the ENT trio doing?" Zayd asked with a wink, referring to Danya, Mia, and Mira.

Danya smiled, her heart swelling with pride. "We're doing just fine, Zayd. Keeping things together as always."

He nodded, his eyes glistening with gratitude. "I'm glad to hear it. You all have been my backbone through all of this."

Turning to the History Trio, Zayd's expression grew more serious. "You're the ones who kept things going. Without you, I wouldn't be here."

Naureen, his former student and long-time friend, smiled warmly. "We're all in this together, Zayd. You taught us that."

The bond between them was undeniable. Zayd had not just been a mentor to them professionally but had shaped their lives and careers in ways they couldn't put into words.

As the group continued to talk, Danya stayed quiet for a moment, watching Zayd interact with the others. She stepped closer to his side, reaching out to check his pulse. A small but noticeable flutter Beneath her fingertips caused her to pause.

She could feel it—a steady pulse, strong and firm, despite everything he had been through. It was a sign, a signal that Zayd was truly coming back. She couldn't help but let out a small breath of relief.

Zayd noticed her gesture and looked up at her, his eyes soft. "Don't worry, Danya. I'm not going anywhere."

She smiled at him, her heart full. "I know. You're a fighter, Zayd. Always have been."

The group continued to chat, catching up on everything that had happened, both in the world of medicine and in their personal lives. There was laughter, and even a few tears, but above all, there was a sense of peace. They had all made it through this together.

As the conversation drifted on, Danya couldn't help but think about the road ahead. Zayd was alive, but he still had a long way to go before he could return to his normal life. There would be more tests, more procedures, and more uncertainty. But for now, they could all take comfort in the fact that he had survived.

And for Danya, that was enough. She knew they would face whatever came next together, as a team. Just like they always had.

Danya's Diary

Today has been one of those days when I truly feel the weight of how much my parents' values have shaped me. As I walked out of the hospital, reflecting on everything that's happened in the past few weeks, I couldn't help but think about Amma and Nana. The way they raised me, always teaching me to be kind, considerate, and compassionate, has carried me through so many challenges.

I've always felt proud to carry their legacy, but today, something about the way they expressed their pride in me made it feel different. It's like they can see everything I've accomplished, but they don't just see my career—they see the heart behind it. They've always encouraged me to be the kind of person who lifts others, whether it's through medicine or just showing care when someone needs it.

Amma always says that kindness is one of the most important things we can give to others. I try my best to live by that, especially in the busy chaos of my work. It's not always easy, but I always come back to those words. Today, in particular, I thought about how Zayd has been there for all of us, how he taught us everything, and how we, in turn, are able to help others because of him. I see the ripple effect of kindness and mentorship—just like Amma and Nana showed me.

Even when things are overwhelming, I try to be present and do what I can for others, not just because it's my Job, but because it's who I am. Seeing my parents light up with pride when I call them—when I tell them about the difference I can make in people's lives—reminds me of how much they've instilled in me. I can see it in their eyes when they talk about how proud they are of what I've achieved. It's humbling and comforting at the same time.

It's not just about being a good doctor; it's about being a good person. And as I continue on this Journey, I carry their lessons with me. The legacy of kindness, patience, and care isn't just something they gave me—it's something I'm now passing on to others, just like they passed it on to me.

Nihal? Well, he was so proud of me. He treated me to authentic Burmese takeout, like we did when we first met. He is just the sweetest, bravest and best husband I can imagine. He is a wonderful father to our little ones.

I can't help but think how lucky I am to have had such wonderful role models in my life. They've shaped me into the person I am today, and now, I get to pass that legacy on, both to my patients and my colleagues.

I hope one day, when my children are older, they'll look back and see that same sense of pride in the values I passed down to them. The kind of legacy that never really ends—it only grows.

Chapter 26: Legal Action Against the Wongs

The day the lawsuit was filed felt surreal to Danya. It wasn't about the money—no amount of money could undo what had happened, and no amount could bring back the trust that had been broken. But it was about justice, about showing that what the Wongs had done was not just unethical, but criminal. Their deception had gone on for far too long, and now it was time for them to face the consequences.

Danya stood beside Mia, Mira, and the rest of the ENT team in the courtroom, facing the judge. They had worked together for years, saving lives, protecting their patients, and ensuring that no one else would suffer from the Wongs' lies. They knew they had a responsibility to speak out, not just for their own careers, but for the future of their profession.

As the judge entered the room, the air grew heavy with anticipation. Everyone in the room knew the gravity of what was about to unfold. The Wongs sat at the opposite end of the room, looking remarkably different from the confident, self-assured doctors they had once pretended to be. They now looked like ordinary people caught in a web of lies, their once pristine reputations shattered.

Danya felt her heart racing. It had taken months of work—gathering evidence, working with the police, and pushing through their own doubts—but today, they were here. The ENT team, along with their colleagues from the History trio, the Radiology team, and all the other professionals who had been involved, were ready to testify.

The prosecutor stood first. "Your Honor, we are here today to seek justice for the Wongs' actions. Dr. Alex Wong and Dr. Anya Wong, pretending to be oncologists, have not only manipulated their way into the medical community but have also endangered the lives of countless patients, including Dr. Zayd Hasan."

Danya's thoughts immediately went to Zayd. The man who had mentored her, who had been a guiding light in her life and in her career. He wasn't just a colleague—he was family. The deception had almost cost him everything. But now, he was recovering, and his fight for survival would not be in vain.

"We will show that Dr. Alex Wong and Dr. Anya Wong were responsible for falsifying their credentials, manipulating medical records, and poisoning Dr. Hasan with toxins that put him into a coma. These actions were deliberate and intentional."

Mia stepped forward to give her statement. "Your Honor, as a colleague and someone who has worked alongside Dr. Zayd Hasan for years, I can testify to the significant harm caused by the Wongs. Not only did they infiltrate the medical community under false pretences, but they also caused a direct and dangerous impact on Dr. Hasan's health. They deliberately put his life in jeopardy, and for that, they must be held accountable."

The judge nodded, acknowledging Mia's statement. Then, Mira spoke up, her voice calm but firm. "I've worked with Dr. Zayd Hasan for years. He is not just a colleague, but a friend. The Wongs' actions were not just a breach of trust—they were criminal. The toxins they administered to him were a direct cause of the coma he fell into. If not for the quick response from our team, he may not have survived."

Danya stood tall next, her voice unwavering. "As a member of the ENT team and someone who has known Dr. Hasan both personally and professionally for years, I can say with certainty that the Wongs' actions were intentional and malicious. Their actions put a respected doctor's life in danger. Their frauds infiltrated our community, and we need to ensure that no one else falls victim to their lies."

The judge turned to address the Wongs directly. "Dr. Alex Wong and Dr. Anya Wong, you have been accused of impersonating medical professionals, falsifying your credentials, and endangering the life of Dr. Zayd Hasan. What do you have to say for yourselves?"

The Wongs exchanged uneasy glances. Alex Wong opened his mouth to speak, but no words came out. Anya Wong, usually so confident, now seemed small and vulnerable. After a long pause, Alex spoke, his voice shaky. "We—uh—we didn't mean for things to go this far. We didn't mean to hurt anyone."

But the judge wasn't swayed. "You didn't just 'go too far.' You consciously made decisions that put lives at risk. This is a Matter of life and death, and your actions will have consequences."

The Wongs fell silent, knowing they had no defence. It was too late to undo what they had done.

After the court proceedings, the team gathered together outside the courthouse, reflecting on what had just transpired. Zayd had been called in to testify as well, but his recovery was still in its early stages, so he had sent a statement instead. They all knew that today wasn't about celebrating their victory—it was about ensuring that justice was done.

Danya received a message from her family soon after. Amma and Nana, along with her brothers and Meera, had flown over to the UK. It was a bittersweet feeling, knowing that the case was finally being addressed, but also feeling the weight of everything they had gone through.

As Danya walked out of the courthouse, her phone rang. It was Zayd, calling from his recovery room. She stepped aside to answer, unable to keep the smile from her face.

"Danya," Zayd's voice crackled through the line, "I know this has been a tough time for all of you, but I want to thank you. Not just for helping me recover, but for fighting for what's right. I couldn't have asked for a better team to be there for me."

"Zayd," Danya responded, her voice thick with emotion, "we did this together. You taught us all so much, and now we're making sure that no one else has to go through what you did."

As Danya ended the call, she stood still for a moment, taking it all in. The battle wasn't over yet. There would be more legal battles, more challenges to face. But today, they had taken a step toward justice.

Back at the hospital, there was still work to do. The ENT team was needed in the green area, as always. But now, there was a sense of closure—a sense that, no Matter how long it had taken, the Wongs had been held accountable for their actions.

And for Zayd, for their team, and for everyone who had been affected, that was enough.

Later that evening, the ENT team gathered together for dinner, Joined by their families, the History trio, and even Prekshya, who had been with them from the very start of the investigation. They shared stories, laughter, and a sense of unity that had never been stronger. There was still a long road ahead, but for the first time in a while, they allowed themselves to feel the weight of their hard work lifting, even if just for a moment.

The night was quiet, but the peace felt earned.

Danya's Diary

It's hard to believe that it's all finally over. The Wongs have been arrested, and the case is moving toward its conclusion. Everyone has been talking about it, of course. It's been a whirlwind of emotions, and I still can't quite process everything that's happened.

It feels so strange to think about everything that led to this moment. When we first started uncovering the truth, I was just trying to do what I do best—helping my patients and doing everything I could to support my team. But then the Wongs came into the picture, and things went from routine to a full-blown crisis in the blink of an eye.

I can still hear Zayd's voice on the phone when I told him the news. His words were so simple, but they meant so much: "You fought for what's right." Sometimes it doesn't feel like it was just me fighting. It was all of us—Mia, Mira, and everyone else in our team, not to mention the History trio, the radiologists, and even Prekshya. It was a whole team effort, and without their support, I don't think we would have been able to bring the Wongs to justice.

I'm glad that we did what was necessary. But there's also this sense of relief now. I can see the tension in everyone's faces starting to ease. There's still a lot of work to be done, and the legal battles aren't over yet, but we've taken the first big step.

As for Zayd, he's doing better. I can feel a little bit of hope now that he's out of the coma. I still can't believe how close we came to losing him. He's been such a guiding force in my life and in the lives of so many others. He's more than just a colleague to me—he's a mentor, a friend, and someone who has shaped who I am as a doctor.

When I saw him again, it was surreal. Seeing him in the recovery room was a mixture of emotions. I wanted to feel happy that he was alive, but at the same time, all I could think about was the fact that the

Wongs had tried to take him away from us. The anger still simmers, but I know that now, it's about moving forward.

Mia and Mira were by my side, just like they've always been. They've been through so much with me, and I honestly don't know where I'd be without them. The three of us—along with Zayd, of course—formed something special over the years, and I don't think anything will ever change that.

And then there's my family. I'm so grateful for their unwavering support, especially Amma and Nana. It's been such a strange time, and there have been so many moments when I've felt overwhelmed. But they've always been there for me, keeping me grounded.

Tomorrow, the legal proceedings will continue, and we'll be doing more work in the hospital, but for tonight, I'm just going to let myself breathe. We've come so far, and although the Journey isn't over, we've accomplished something significant.

It's been a difficult road, but I know that with my team by my side and the people I love supporting me, we'll make it through. We always do.

Chapter 27: Peace at last

The sun had barely set, casting a golden hue over the garden outside Zayd's house. It felt like the world had finally exhaled after a long, drawn-out breath. The trials, the investigation, the uncertainty—it all seemed like a distant memory now. Tonight, it was a celebration, and everything was back in its rightful place.

The invitation to Zayd's house had been extended to everyone who had been part of the Journey—Danya's colleagues, friends, and even her family. The air was thick with joy, laughter, and the comforting sound of clinking glasses. It was a moment to forget the weight of the last few months and simply enjoy being together.

Danya's parents, Amma and Nana, had flown in from India for the occasion, eager to see their daughter and celebrate the happiness that had returned to their lives. It wasn't just any celebration—it was also Zayd and Evelyn's golden wedding anniversary. Fifty years of love, dedication, and partnership. A remarkable milestone for a remarkable couple. Danya felt a deep sense of gratitude, both for her own family and for Zayd's.

Zayd's children—Samira, the eldest, and her younger sister Sara—were there too, along with their spouses and children. Danya's younger siblings, Arjun and Meera, had arrived earlier, and now they were all gathered in Zayd's spacious living room, chatting animatedly with everyone.

The evening began with speeches, as expected, and Zayd stood up first, raising his glass. His voice, although softer than before, carried a warmth and wisdom that filled the room.

"Thank you all for being here tonight," he began. "We've been through so much together, and the support you've given Evelyn and me over the years has been invaluable. But tonight, let's focus on the good—the people we've helped, the lives we've touched, and the family we've built."

Evelyn smiled beside him, her hand resting gently on his. "I couldn't have asked for a better partner in life. And tonight, we celebrate not just fifty years of marriage, but the love and Joy that we continue to share with all of you."

Danya's heart swelled with pride as she watched them. Zayd had been through so much—his medical battles, the fake oncologists, the coma—but here he was, stronger than ever, with Evelyn by his side.

As the speeches came to an end, Danya found herself surrounded by her family and friends. Her parents were chatting happily with Mia and Mira, laughing at something Samira had said. Arjun and Meera were deep in conversation with Elodie and Kanchana, discussing their latest academic projects. It felt like home—a sense of belonging that was hard to find in the midst of everything that had happened.

The evening continued with food, music, and heartfelt toasts. Zayd and Evelyn's golden anniversary was marked with a cake—something extravagant, with layers of frosting and delicate gold accents that sparkled in the light. Danya, still in awe of the moment, found herself sitting with her parents, watching as they shared stories of her childhood, of the days before she entered medicine, when things were simpler.

"Danya," Amma said softly, her eyes glistening with pride. "I always knew you would do great things. You've always been determined, always so compassionate. It's so good to see you surrounded by people who respect and admire you."

Nana nodded, his deep voice filled with warmth. "You've done well, my daughter. You've taken everything life has thrown at you, and you've kept your heart strong."

Danya smiled, feeling the weight of her parents' words settle over her like a comforting blanket. "It's all been worth it, Amma, Nana. Every challenge, every moment of doubt—it's led me to this point. And now, I'm grateful to have all of you with me."

Later in the evening, after the last toast had been made, Danya found herself standing by the window with Zayd. The sky had darkened, and the stars were beginning to twinkle above. They stood there in quiet contemplation, watching as the last of the guests mingled in the garden.

"I never thought we'd make it this far," Zayd said, his voice soft but steady. "It's been a long road. But I'm proud of what we've done. Proud of you, Danya. You've always had a way of making things right."

Danya felt a lump form in her throat. She didn't often hear words like that from Zayd, and to hear them now, after everything that had happened, meant more than she could express.

"You're my mentor," she replied, her voice thick with emotion. "You taught me how to be the doctor I am today. I wouldn't have made it without you."

He smiled, his tired eyes sparkling with a mix of gratitude and affection. "You did all the hard work, Danya. But I'm glad I was there to guide you along the way. And now, look at where we are. We've come full circle."

The night ended on a high note, with everyone feeling content, their hearts full of Joy. Zayd, Evelyn, and their children were surrounded by the people who Mattered most to them. For the first time in a long while, there was a deep sense of peace in the air.

As Danya lay in bed later that night, reflecting on everything that had led to this moment, she felt a sense of quiet accomplishment. The world was still full of challenges, but for tonight, they could rest easy. Everything was back at peace.

And for that, she was eternally grateful.

Danya's Diary

The past few days have felt like a whirlwind of emotions. So much has happened, but at the same time, everything feels calm and peaceful now. The hospital, the surgeries, the investigation, and all the chaos leading up to this point—it's all behind us.

Tonight, we celebrated Zayd's golden wedding anniversary, and I couldn't have imagined a more beautiful evening. Being surrounded by friends, family, and colleagues who have become like family was everything I needed. It's amazing to see how far we've come, not just with Zayd's recovery but with everything that's happened in the last few months.

Amma and Nana came over from India to join the celebration, and it meant the world to me. I could see how proud they were of me, not just for what I've achieved in my career but for the person I've become. They always knew I could do great things, but hearing them say it again, after everything we've been through, just made my heart swell.

Zayd and Evelyn were glowing tonight. Fifty years of marriage, fifty years of love, support, and dedication. They've been through so much together, and it was beautiful to see them celebrate this milestone surrounded by so many who care about them. I think about everything that happened—Zayd's coma, the fraud with the Wongs, all the investigations—and I can hardly believe it's over. It feels like a lifetime ago, yet it feels like we've only just begun.

The party itself was full of joy, laughter, and good food. Everyone was talking, laughing, and sharing stories. Zayd gave a touching speech, and Evelyn followed with words that came from the heart. It's hard to imagine what they've been through, but they came out of it stronger than ever. They're a testament to resilience, love, and the importance of never giving up.

I spent some time with Amma and Nana, sharing old memories. I don't often talk about my childhood with them, but tonight felt like the right time. It made me realise how much they've always been there for me, even when I didn't fully appreciate it. Their unwavering belief in me has been a constant source of strength.

After the speeches, we all enjoyed the evening, talking and catching up. Zayd and Evelyn's anniversary cake was the highlight, covered in gold accents that sparkled under the lights. There was so much warmth in the room, so much love. I think that's what I'll remember most—how we all came together, how we supported each other, and how we celebrated life.

As I stood with Zayd later in the evening, watching the guests mingle in the garden, I couldn't help but reflect on how far we've come. It's been a difficult road, but we've all learned so much. Zayd and I spoke quietly, and for the first time in a while, I felt like everything was in its right place.

I've never been one to dwell on the past, but tonight I allowed myself to take it all in—to appreciate how far we've come, and how much we've all grown. Zayd said something that stuck with me: "We've come full circle." It's true. From the uncertainty and fear of the past months to this peaceful moment, it feels like a new chapter has begun.

I don't know what the future holds, but tonight I'm just going to savour this. Tomorrow is another day, but for tonight, I'll rest easy knowing that things are finally back in place.

Amma, Nana, and my siblings are here, and that makes everything even better. The warmth of their presence is comforting, and I'm so thankful to have them in my life.

Zayd and Evelyn's celebration was perfect, and it's just the beginning of the peace for which we've all been waiting. I hope we can carry this calm with us as we move forward. There's so much still ahead, but tonight, I'm at peace.

I couldn't have asked for a better way to end this chapter.

Epilogue: One Year Later

It had been one year since everything had settled down—the chaos, the investigations, the surgeries, the challenges. Now, life had returned to a rhythm of peace, and it was time for a new chapter, one filled with Joy and celebration.

Ravi's wedding to Kajal had brought the whole family together in Delhi, and the occasion was nothing short of magical. The preparations had been extensive, with relatives flying in from all over, and Danya, of course, was right at the heart of it all. She and her family were still riding the high of the events from the year before, and now they had something to celebrate that was so full of love.

Danya had invited the history trio—Naureen, Kanchana, and Elodie—along with her closest colleagues from the ENT team: Mira, Mia, and Zayd. Laila, Zayd's sister and his wife, had also flown in, along with Samira and her younger sister Sara. Omar and Rami, as always, were part of the team, and everyone was thrilled to come together for this Joyful occasion.

The wedding ceremony itself was everything Danya could have hoped for. It was a beautiful traditional affair, with vibrant colours, intricate decorations, and a sense of warmth that filled the entire venue. Ravi and Kajal looked radiant, both of them glowing with happiness as they exchanged vows. Their love was palpable, and it was impossible not to feel the sheer Joy that surrounded them.

For Danya, it was a reminder of how life had changed in such a short amount of time. One year ago, everything had seemed uncertain, and now, here they were—surrounded by family, friends, and a sense of belonging that was unshakeable. There was laughter, music, and dancing, with everyone enjoying the celebration together.

The ENT trio and the history trio had spent the evening reminiscing about their shared experiences, how they'd stood together through the most challenging of times. Zayd was a constant source of Joy and conversation, and Danya felt the familiar sense of comfort whenever they spoke. The bond they shared was undeniable, and it was clear that no Matter how much time had passed, they would always be a part of each other's lives.

Mira and Mia were with Danya throughout the evening, laughing and teasing each other as they made their way from table to table. The warmth of their friendship was like a steady flame, something Danya had come to rely on, especially after the storms they had weathered together.

Laila, Samira, and Sara were all thrilled to see each other again, and it was clear that the ties between their families had only strengthened with time. Zayd, ever the supportive figure, beamed with pride as he watched his sister and nieces enjoy themselves.

The night ended with a huge celebration—music, dancing, and laughter echoing through the halls. Danya couldn't remember the last time she had enjoyed herself so much. Ravi's wedding had brought everyone closer, and it was the perfect way to mark a fresh start for all of them. There was so much ahead, but for tonight, everyone was just grateful for the Joy they had.

As the evening wound down, Danya found herself standing with her family—Amma and Nana, Ravi and Kajal, and all her closest friends. She couldn't help but feel a deep sense of gratitude. Looking around at the people who had supported her, loved her, and been there for her through everything, Danya knew that the future was bright.

One year later, the Journey they had been on was no longer just about survival—it was about living. And she couldn't have asked for anything more.

Danya's Memoir

It's hard to believe how much has changed in just a year. A year ago, I was in the midst of something I never expected—a whirlwind of chaos, mystery, and uncertainty. But now, sitting here, reflecting on everything that has transpired, I can't help but feel a sense of peace and gratitude. Life has a way of surprising us, and sometimes, those surprises bring about the most unexpected blessings.

The Journey began with the people who had always been a part of my life—my teachers, my mentors, my friends. Zayd and Laila were more than just colleagues to me; they were like family. They were the ones who shaped me, who guided me through the toughest of times. They taught me everything I knew, not just about medicine, but about life, about perseverance, about the power of compassion. Alongside them, I had the privilege of learning from others—Naureen, Mira, Kanchana, Elodie, and Mia. We were all connected, united by the same passion for knowledge and for helping others. Zayd and Laila's lessons went far beyond textbooks. They taught us how to care, how to listen, how to truly make a difference in the lives of others.

But it wasn't just the lessons that defined us; it was the bond we shared. As a group, we had weathered storms, faced challenges, and fought for what was right. The memories of those times still linger—when we worked together to unravel the mysteries surrounding Zayd's supposed death, when we fought for justice, and when we finally came together to see Zayd restored. It was a reminder that, no Matter the obstacles, we could overcome anything as long as we had each other.

When Zayd was first taken from us, it felt like the world had turned upside down. It wasn't as sad as losing my grandparents but it still tore me. It wasn't just the shock of what happened to him; it was the sense of helplessness that came with it. We were all in disbelief. How could something so wrong happen to someone so good? Zayd had always been the one who took care of others, who protected us, who guided us with his wisdom. And yet, there he was—fighting for his life. But even in that darkness, there was a flicker of hope. We never gave up on him, and eventually, that hope became a reality.

I'll never forget the moment when we found out the truth. The Wongs, those who had pretended to be oncologists, had poisoned Zayd. They had tried to take him away from us. It was hard to process, hard to believe that such malice could exist in the world. But, in the end, justice prevailed. The Wongs were exposed, arrested, and taken down for their crimes. It wasn't about the money. It was never about the money. It was about doing what was right, about making sure Zayd's name was cleared, and that those responsible for trying to take him away from us faced the consequences of their actions.

The lawsuits, the investigation, the emotional toll it took on us all—it was something we would never forget. But through it all, we stood by each other. The ENT team, the history trio, Zayd's family—we were all in this together. And in the end, that's what Mattered. We didn't just recover from the ordeal; we grew stronger. Stronger in our resolve, stronger in our commitment to each other and to the people we served.

And now, a year later, here we are—celebrating life, celebrating love, and celebrating the people who mean the most to us. Ravi's wedding to Kajal was the perfect way to mark this new chapter in our lives. It was a celebration of not just their love, but of everything we had been through to get here. My parents, my siblings, my closest friends—all of us gathered together to witness something beautiful. Ravi had found his soulmate, and I couldn't be happier for him. It was a reminder that life, even in its darkest moments, has a way of bringing light into our lives.

At the wedding, I couldn't help but reflect on everything that had happened—the challenges, the triumphs, the friendships. Zayd and Laila had taught us so much, not just in the medical field, but in life.

They had shown us that even in the face of adversity, we could rise above. And now, we were here, celebrating the love and the bonds that had carried us through.

Mira, Mia, Naureen, Kanchana, Elodie—we were all there, together, once again. The ENT trio, the history trio—we had been through so much, and now we were stronger than ever. It was a beautiful thing, to be surrounded by people who had been there for you through thick and thin. We had become a family, in the truest sense of the word.

The Joy at Ravi's wedding was contagious. Laughter filled the air, music echoed through the halls, and there was a sense of happiness that seemed to radiate from every corner of the room. Zayd, always the pillar of strength, was there with his family, smiling and enjoying the moment. His recovery had been nothing short of miraculous, and we were all so thankful to see him happy, healthy, and whole again.

As I stood there, surrounded by the people I loved, I realized how far we had come. A year ago, we were struggling to make sense of the events that had turned our lives upside down. Now, we were standing together, stronger than ever, ready to face whatever came next. And in that moment, I knew that no Matter what life threw at our way, we would always have each other. We would always rise above, because that's what we had learned—together, we could overcome anything.

Looking around at my family, my friends, my colleagues, I couldn't help but feel an overwhelming sense of gratitude. Life had a way of testing us, of challenging us in ways we never expected. But it had also shown us the power of love, of friendship, and of resilience. We had faced the worst and come out stronger, together. And now, as we celebrated this new chapter in our lives, I knew that nothing could ever break the bond we shared. The future was bright, and I was ready to embrace it, surrounded by the people who Mattered most.

Acknowledgements

First and foremost, I want to thank my family, especially my parents, for their unwavering support and love. Their encouragement and belief in me have made everything possible. You have always been my rock, and I am incredibly grateful for everything you've done for me.

A special mention goes to my late grandfather, Balasubramaniam. Although you are no longer here with us, your wisdom and guidance continue to inspire me. Your legacy lives on, and I will forever carry your teachings with me.

To my friends—thank you for being there through every step of this Journey. Your friendship means the world to me, and I couldn't have asked for a better support system. You have all been a source of inspiration and motivation, and I'm so thankful for each and every one of you.

To my teachers, especially in the history department, I want to express my deepest gratitude. Your encouragement to continue with *Once Upon Historians* and take it even further into this book means so much. I appreciate all the knowledge you've imparted, and your support has helped me grow not just as a student but as a person.

Thank you also to my Year 10 friends who contributed and helped bring this story to life. The characters based on real people, like Alex and Anya Wong, are not a reflection of those individuals. You know who you are, and I'm so grateful for your kindness and input. Your creativity has added so much to this Journey.

Lastly, I would like to thank Draft2Digital and all of their distributors for helping with the publishing and cover art. Your professional expertise and hard work have made this project come to life in ways I never imagined.

Thank you all for making this possible and for believing in this story. Without all of you, this book would not have been the same.

About the Author

Danika, a 13-year-old bookworm, has always been passionate about reading and writing. As she delved deeper into her studies, her love for learning only grew stronger. She spent hours devouring books of all genres, and soon discovered that she had a knack for storytelling herself. With the encouragement of her teachers and family, Danika began writing her own tales, weaving intricate plots and characters that came alive on the page. Her hard work paid off when she published her first book, "Once Upon Historians", a historical fiction novel that combines her love of reading and learning. Through writing, Danika finds solace and escape from the stresses of everyday life, using her words as a tool to cope with her emotions and process her thoughts. With "Once Upon Historians" under her belt, Danika is determined to continue pursuing her dreams and inspiring others to do the same. Danika, a 13-year-old bookworm, has always been passionate about reading and writing. As she delved deeper into her studies, her love for learning only grew stronger. She spent hours devouring books of all genres, and soon discovered that she had a knack for storytelling herself. With the encouragement of her teachers and family, Danika began writing her own tales, weaving intricate plots and characters that came alive on the page. Her hard work paid off when she published her first book, "Once Upon Historians", a historical fiction novel that combines her love of reading and learning. Through writing, Danika finds solace and escape from the stresses of everyday life, using her words as a tool to cope with her emotions and process her thoughts. With "Once Upon Historians" under her belt, Danika is determined to continue pursuing her dreams and inspiring others to do the same.

www.ingramcontent.com/pod-product-compliance
Ingram Content Group UK Ltd.
Pitfield, Milton Keynes, MK11 3LW, UK
UKHW040724190225
455309UK00001B/42